Wind-Up Toy: Broken Plaything

David Owain Hughes

Including Happy Birthday, Simone and Playtime, Simone.

WIND-UP TOY: BROKEN PLAYTHING

DAVID OWAIN HUGHES

INCLUDING HAPPY BIRTHDAY, SIMONE AND PLAYTIME, SIMONE.

Darkerwood Publishing Group
Colorado, U.S.A.

Darkerwood Publishing Group
Colorado, U.S.A.
First Paperback Printing, June 2016 - U.S.A.

ISBN: 978-0-9788975-9-8

Cover art by Kevin Enhart

See the back of this book for more information about the author and his work.

Dedication

For Richard Laymon

STORIES IN THE WIND-UP TOY SERIES

Wind-Up Toy
Happy Birthday, Simone
Playtime, Simone
Broken Plaything
Chaos Rising

WIND-UP TOY: BROKEN PLAYTHING

"Forgive me Father, for I have sinned…" Simone said, bowing his head.

"How long since your last confession, my child?"

"More years than I care to remember, Father."

"And what have you to confess, my son…?"

***

By the time Simone got to his front door, he'd managed to stop giggling like a little schoolgirl, but the lopsided grin still remained – it was cartoonish in size, which, in turn, displayed his well-polished teeth and healthy gums.

"That's a real shit-eating grin you have there, love…" he could hear his mother say. She had one of the most radiant smiles he'd ever seen, and he couldn't wait to tell her what the women down at Bunnies had given him today for his twentieth birthday, which had been yesterday.

A belated gift, but still – it had been amazing.

1

The lovelies at his mother's workplace had lined up and given him a lap dance followed by a striptease. The manager, a close friend of his mother's, had even closed the place for a few hours so Simone could enjoy his birthday treat.

At the back of his mind, he knew she had probably sucked his dick to get it to happen, but he was cool with it. She loved him, as he did her, and so he let things like that slide. His mother was an adult. A beautiful woman who knew what she was doing.

Oh, if only Mr. Tickles had been there! he thought.

Crystal, his favourite, had lingered, and taken her time rubbing her arse against his dick, which had been a solid pillar beneath his trousers. When she was finished teasing, her striptease had been equally slow.

Simone, who had already blown his load twice, came a third time to Crystal and her performance.

What a woman, he thought, pushing his front door wide open. As he entered the hallway, a blast of music hit him. His smile grew wider. It was coming from his mother's dance room...*A final belated show for my birthday? She's such a wonderful mother. Maybe after her performance, she will want to take a shower with me! A bath is nice, but a shower is even better – her rubdowns are heavenly.*

When he got to the foot of the stairs, he looked up and called to his mother, but she didn't hear. Either that, or she did hear and wasn't answering. That was her way of telling him she wanted to be spied on, wanted his eyes on her.

He wasn't one for refusing either. Since he'd come of age, she'd relaxed about him watching her. He didn't have to peep any longer, but, like him, she knew half the thrill was in peeping from a hidden place.

Oh, Mam… he thought, excitement building in him.

After removing his shoes and coat and placing his keys on the hook close to the front door, Simone sauntered into the living room. All the lights were off, but he could still see. The afternoon sun may have been dying, but it was enough to light his path as he looked for Mr. Tickles.

I'm sure I left…

'Here, sir!' the clown called out.

"There you are!" Simone said, picking up his toy clown from the sofa. "You missed a treat at Bunnies, Mr. Tickles. Mam arranged a special show for me down there."

'Those dirty fuckers get their titties out for you, sir?!'

"Oh, yes! You should have seen the show Crystal gave me, man…Rubbed her arse, tits and *bush* in my face and crotch. It was amazing. She didn't hold back. None of them did, to be fair."

'Mother's in her dance room! Shall we…?'

Simone's smile grew wide once more as he clutched his clown close to his chest and marched upstairs.

'The new peephole, sir?'

"Hmm, why not!" Simone said. When he reached the second floor, he took a right and headed into the room directly in front of him. Opening the door, he looked inside before entering. Over the years, this space had become a dumping ground. It housed his old toys, clothes and some of his mother's costumes.

Before it had become like this, it had acted as Sian's room. Oh, how he'd had fun playing in this bedroom with her. But that was a long time ago now, and all he had left were memories of his sister.

3

Last month, when snooping around in here, Simone had stumbled into her walk-in wardrobe and discovered some plaster missing off the back wall. On further inspection, with prodding and picking, he'd opened up a hole. On looking through it, he pleasantly noticed he could see directly into his mother's dance room.

Having thought all the walls in his mother's room were sound proofed, he'd checked one night when she was out and discovered that the section supporting the hole was in fact missing some padding.

He used this to his advantage. The ceiling hole had become boring since his mother knew that's where he always spied from, even though she knew he was doing it, something was removed from the peeping. The game. The façade that he and her played.

With a new hole in place, he could get excited about watching her again – she may have known his eyes were on her, but she didn't know from where they watched. It was hot. Erotic, even. It made his dick twice as solid, which impressed her.

"You don't think it's a small one?" he'd asked her last year, after a girl had laughed at him.

"No, honey, not at all. It's a very nice penis," she'd assured him.

Of course, some of the girls down at Bunnies had also assured Simone about his size. Not that women laughing at it bothered him. He found the experience rather kinky.

Once, one summer ago, a girl had laughed at his semi-hard cock under the pier down on the beach. At the time, he couldn't understand why he hadn't slugged her in the face, then kicked her ribs to dust when she was down, but the moment had thrilled him – his cock had grown in his hand, much to her fright.

"You're fucking weird!" she declared before storming off.

He'd pleaded with her to stay, to tough it out, but she'd thrown sand in his face and run away. "I'm going to tell my dad on you!" had been her parting words.

"Fucking tell, you whore!" had been his to her, as he'd spat crunchy, golden particles from his mouth.

Stepping into the room, he drew in a deep breath. Even though it had been years since Sian had occupied the room, he could still smell her. He found that extraordinary really. How could it be possible? It didn't matter, because he could.

Her womanly scent and perfume clung to the air like a ghost.

"I miss you so much…" he whispered.

'Chin up, sir. Mam is waiting!'

"You always know how to cheer me up, don't you?"

'Affirmative, sir –it's how you brought me and the other guys up. Krull army would be nothing without you and your discipline, sir.'

"Well, you're a good number two, Mr. Tickles," he told the stuffed toy as he held it from his body.

The clown nodded.

To Simone's surprise, the music in the opposite room came to a long silence.

The CD has probably finished, he thought. *Any minute now, I'll hear her change the disc…*

But it never came.

Intrigued, Simone quickened his pace and moved to the wardrobe. Upon opening the doors, the hole winked at him as light from behind it shone through. He moved forward and placed his eye against it.

She was nowhere to be seen.

Odd...

His heart started to race. Was she playing tricks on him? Was she hiding, about to jump out and scare him? She was prone to do such things. His smile returned. His hard-on faltered.

"Come on, you prick tease..."

'Anything, sir?'

Simone shook his head, about to speak, then the music kicked back in – Nazareth were singing about love hurting.

Getting onto tiptoes, Simone cast his eyeball downward. Nothing. Then he looked as far left as he could. Nothing. Before totally giving in, he shot his eye right, and that's when he saw her.

She was lying on the floor, her stiff nipples pointing at Simone's peephole in the ceiling directly above her.

A laugh escaped him. "What silly game is she up to now?!" he said, sniggering all the while. His shoulders skipped with his hearty chuckles.

'What is it, sir?'

"It's Mam, she's..." Then, something odd about her positioning struck him. Her left leg was bent at an awkward angle beneath her, as though she had collapsed onto it. Her arms were stretched out at her sides, with one slightly bent at the elbow.

He didn't know if it was his imagination or not, but he couldn't see the rise and fall of her stomach.

"Mam..." he said, sounding warbly. Tears were threatening. "Mammy?!" Simone's voice cracked. Mucus clogged his throat, stopping him from saying another word.

'Sir?' Mr. Tickles said.

Simone didn't answer. He exited the wardrobe as fast as he could, almost tripping over some of the junk which lay scattered about his feet.

"No..." he finally managed, wiping some of the tears off his cheeks, which were spilling from his eyes in abundance. "Please, no...Not her!"

Leaving the spare room, he went to her door and hammered his fist against it. When she didn't answer or open up for him, his fears were as good as confirmed – she was dead.

Trying the door handle, he found it locked.

"Mam!" he screamed. The tears leaking from him blurred his vision. "*Mammy!*"

Stepping back, he raised his leg and smashed his foot against the lock. Wood splintered with a sickening snap, but the door stood firm. Retracting his leg, he kicked out again. This time, the handle fell off the door and it opened a crack.

Pushing it fully open, a breath hitched in his throat – he was too terrified to look inside, but he knew he had to. After all, she could just be sleeping.

Maybe she's fainted?

Walking into the room, Simone went to the CD player and turned it off.

"Mam?" he called. He sniffled and wiped the tears from his cheeks. "*Mam?!*" His bottom lip trembled.

'Sir, maybe we should call for help?'

Ignoring Mr. Tickles, Simone edged closer and closer to his mother. He could feel his heart crumble beneath his ribcage. His skin turned cold. The hairs at his nape and on his arms stood on end.

He gulped. Hard.

When he got to her side, he put his fingers to the side of her neck – there was no pulse. To double check, he put his ear to her nostrils. She wasn't breathing.

"*Mammy!*" he screeched, scooping her body up in his arms and pressing her tightly to his chest. That was when he saw the multiple bottles of pills sprinkled across the floor like tossed confetti.

Mixed among the tablet containers were stray pills and a smashed glass.

His vision glazed over as he continued to scream and cry hysterically – his whole body shook.

"Wake up, mammy! *Please*, wake up!"

'*Sir, try and calm yourself!*'

Putting her back down, he stood up and started lashing out – he put his fists and feet through her mirrors. He swept all her items off a dressing table she kept in the room. Make-up containers, brushes, wigs, fake eyelashes and nails, lipsticks and a mirror were thrown across the room.

The sound of smashing glass was deafening.

He roared like a jungle warrior and beat his chest like a gorilla. With all his might, he ripped his t-shirt to ribbons.

Finally, out of breath, he collapsed at her side.

"Why?!" he blubbered.

Her once pretty face had turned an ugly chalk-white and her previously rich red kissable lips had been replaced by a sickly blue-purple hue.

Looking down at her, he couldn't believe she was gone. Simone refused to let the information sink in, and, in his stubbornness, he leaned in and kissed her on the mouth.

The iciness he found there stirred something within him.

His loss and heartache was suddenly replaced by anger. Pulling back, he looked into her unblinking eyes.

"You were my world. How could you have done this?!" Rage coursed through him again. "You've betrayed me. Left me alone in this hateful world. Why?!"

He sucked up his tears and refused to spill any more over a woman he had given himself to.

"I loved you so dearly..."

He could feel spite working its way into his brain as his fingers fumbled at the button of her hot pants. Managing to unclasp it, he pulled the denims down her tight-covered thighs and tossed them to one side.

He ran both his hands over her legs and found the fabric to be most pleasing to his touch. His dick stiffened.

"Must I show you how much you mean to me?!" He slapped his dead mother across her cool cheek. "Fucking answer me!"

'Do it, sir – drill her fucking arse to the floorboards! We've waited to feel the inside of that pussy for a long time!'

"Her legs feel so good!" he said, then savagely tore the tights asunder. The horrific sound pleased him, and he smiled harder when he realised she wasn't wearing panties.

Before mounting her tiny frame, he ripped her flimsy bra apart, which exposed her small tits. Her nipples still stood erect.

He licked his lips and then turned her head so he could look into her eyes as he fucked her.

Once he was on her, he pushed his hardness into her, and thrust back and forth gently.

"I love you!" he said, feeling his orgasm quickly building...

"You *screwed* your mother?! Sorry, let me rephrase that – you screwed your *dead* mother?!" she said, bringing him out of the memory.

Turning to face her on the bed, he couldn't help but drink the woman in before answering her. *What's her name?* he thought. *Mary? No. Maggie? Mandy! Mandy Tyra. She's five-foot four-inches of pure heaven and legs. And those red fishnets...Damn!*

Her stockings were supported by matching red suspenders and she wore a garter around her left thigh. Beneath the material on the right thigh, Simone could see a tattoo of a large yellow rose. A fat-bodied snake was entwined around the flower of love, and its thorns were ripping into the Cobra's scaly flesh, causing its blood to flow freely.

Moving his eyes to her crotch, he noticed how well groomed it was, as there was only a thin strip of hair to be found. Earlier in the night, when he'd asked her how clean she was 'down there', she had joked with him about how she didn't cut shapes into her bush.

Just above her pubic bone, she sported more ink. This one, however, was not an image, but words. It read, in stunningly crafted calligraphy: *Tunnel of Love.*

Raising his eyes to her navel, he sought out the piercing she had there – a small hoop with a tiny pendant in the shape of a dream catcher.

"Did you hear me?!" she snapped.

But he wasn't paying any attention – her body had him hypnotized, much like it had put him in a trance earlier in the night. *She is beautiful*, he thought. *Such a flat stomach with well-rounded tits* (which were currently hidden beneath a bra that matched the suspenders). *Hang on, no panties? No, of course not – she explained that to me...*

"I never wear them, sailor – they get in the way of fun!" she'd said, winking at him.

Splendid.

"Hey, Simone!" she said, snapping her fingers.

His head shot up, and he found he was looking into her smouldering green eyes. Her medium brown-coloured hair flanked her pretty face, which was scant of make-up. *I hate it when they have so much make-up on, they look like a fucking clown!*

"Yes?" he said.

"I said, you screwed your dead mother?!"

He nodded. "Yeah, that's right," he said, adding, "Multiple times."

"*What*?! Are you fucking crazy? Do you have wires touching?"

"Hey, you said you understood me. That you felt my pain!"

"Yeah, that's before I knew you screwed a dead body. And not just any dead body, but your mother's!"

"You said you'd listen to my problems. That you would help make all my pain go away – that you would love me, and never hurt me..." He started to raise his voice – he could feel his control slipping away.

"Love you?! Are you fucking nuts? I've only just met you...I thought you wanted to come back to this shitty hotel to fuck?! Isn't that why you picked me up at the strip club tonight?"

"No! I was hoping you would sit and listen to me. I wanted to talk. I wanted to—"

11

"Wow, hey, back up. I did sit and listen to you. We had a few slammers at the bar whilst we shot the shit, remember, stud?" she said.

"Yeah, and I thought you were lovely. That's why I brought you back – I wanted to keep talking. In private!"

"We have – you've been telling me how much you liked screwing your dead mother!"

A laugh escaped her, causing him to lash out. He backhanded her off the bed – her small frame crashed down on top of the nightstand. The phone was thrown to the floor, the cord ripped from the jack. Glass exploded under her, which he guessed was the lamp breaking.

He didn't care that she'd laughed. Humiliation had become his friend – it thrilled him when a woman belittled him. But he drew the line at a bitch being nasty about his relationship with his mother.

A bitch who worked a bar at Pole Puss.

Someone who liked nothing more than having strange men shove notes down her flimsy knickers. *I bet she loves the feel of tenners rubbing against her twat.*

"*Ugh!*" Mandy cried, rolling off the wreckage.

He'd been right about the lamp – it lay in hundreds of pieces at her side. Some shards had stabbed into her stomach.

It isn't so perfect now! he thought, ripping the length of wire out of the back of the phone. He wrapped it around his fists, making a garrotte out of it.

"No!" she whimpered. "Don't, please...I've done nothing to you! I have kids!"

"I thought you may have been the *one*, Mandy. I thought I had finally found my new Toni. But no. You bitches are all the same. You fuck us over. None of you are to be trusted."

"Toni?" she gasped.

"Yeah, long story…I haven't really got the time to go into it with you now," he said, wrapping the wire around her throat. He pulled her off the ground and applied as much pressure to the cord as he could.

"Fu…ck….f…fuc….k…" she gasped, spat and wheezed.

"Yeah, fuck. You're right. I fucked my mother until there was nothing left of her to fuck. I fucked her until parts of her started dropping off; until the body was so badly decomposed, I was forced to bury her in the sand at Porthcawl beach…You're the only person I've told. I never even told…*Her* that!"

When Mandy stopped fighting, he threw her body to one side and collapsed onto the bed. He curled up and wept himself to sleep as he gently rocked back and forth.

"Mammy," he blubbered.

***

The priest muttered something before he spoke directly to Simone. "And when was this, my child?"

"Last night, Father…"

"I see. And what did you do next, my son? Did you call the police?"

'No, you fucking retard! We cut that cunt up with a hacksaw, starting with her head, then buried her under the floorboards of the—'

"*Shh*! Mr. Tickles!" Simone said as quiet as he possibly could, covering the clown's mouth with a hand. In the dimly lit confessional box, Simone could just about make out the form of his number two, who sat on his lap facing him. "I don't want to tell him stuff like that!"

13

"Are you okay, my son?"

"Yes, Father – I'm just...I'm feeling slightly overcome by it all," he lied. He fake sobbed.

"Take your time, my boy. There's no rush."

"No, I never alerted the authorities, Father...I was too scared," he lied, again. "After I killed her, I fell asleep. When I woke up the next day, I left the hotel and wandered the streets in the rain for hours before I decided to come here...I didn't know what else to do. I've been so, so bad, Father. I'm scared for my soul. Am I damned?!"

"No, child. Our Lord and saviour loves all his children, even the fallen ones. But, you must do the right thing, my son. You must be able to see that?"

The priest's words struck a chord with Simone, causing genuine tears to roll down his face. *What have I done?* he thought.

"Yes, Father – I know what must be done, but first, I would like to talk to you more. Get things off my chest. Is that okay?"

"Of course, my boy. Here, in the house of our Lord and Father, we have plenty of time for a lost lamb such as yourself."

The Father's warm, tender words helped him to relax.

"Thanks. I need a friendly ear at the moment..."

"Of course. So, child, tell me – who is Toni? You mentioned her when you were telling me about Mandy and your mother."

"Oh, *her*...She's someone I knew. Sadly, she let me down and she's no longer with us. Just like my mother. Betrayed me. I found her in the arms of another. The *bitch* hurt me badly, Father!"

"Please, my boy, if you could refrain from foul language under the Lord's roof..."

"Yes, of course. I'm sorry. I just don't think I'm ready to talk about her just yet, Father."

"That's fine. Tell me what you want, when you want."

"It's their fault I've become this monster, this unholy thing that can't stop hurting people and lusting!"

"Who, child?"

"Women, Father."

"You blame your mother for the bad things you have done?"

"She's one of many, yes."

"Because she failed you as a parent?"

"No, she was a good mother. I blame her for leaving me all alone in this world. She abandoned me – left me to the wolves."

"Why did she do it, son?"

"Take her own life?"

"Yes."

"Because of how I turned out, Father – she blamed my wicked, perverse ways on herself."

"How do you know this?"

"She left a note. It was brief, but to the point."

"I see. That must have been hard on you."

"To this day, I still carry the note, Father. May I read it to you?"

"Of course, my son. But first, tell me: didn't people wonder where your mother had gone to? You never alerted the police of her suicide."

"I told people she had abandoned me, Father. That she had fled back to Italy so she could be with my estranged father."

"I see. Please, read me the letter, son."

"Okay, let me see if I can get to it..." Simone said, standing up and removing his wallet from his back pocket. Before he could sit back down, his mobile started vibrating in his pocket. Digging that out too, he sat back down and opened his phone.

There was a new message awaiting his response.

Hmm, that's odd. I've not had a text or phone call in months. She *was probably one of the last people to text or ring me...*he thought, letting his mind drift as he opened his messages.

When he saw the name, a smile spread across his face. He'd very nearly forgotten about this person, and her friends.

"My God, *Chrissy...*" he whispered.

'Sandoval?' Mr. Tickles piped in. *'Fuck me, that name takes me back, sir.'*

"Yeah, you're not the only one!" Simone said, looking at her message.

'Hey Simone, I hope you still have the same number, and that you receive this message. If you do, long time! I just wanted to let you know that I'm back in Wales with the girls, and I wondered if you'd like to catch up sometime soon?'

'What will you do, sir?'

"I...I'm not sure..."

"Are you okay, my boy?" the priest asked.

"Yes, Father. Could you give me two minutes, please? I'm gathering the strength to read this to you," he lied. Again.

"Of course, my child."

"Chrissy Sandoval," he whispered. He had not uttered her name in at least six years. *She'd always promised to get in touch if she was ever in the area. And by the sounds of things, she's back with her act,* he thought.

***

He couldn't stay inside forever. He knew that, but he couldn't face the world. Now, standing at his front window, Simone peeled the curtains back and looked outside. Summer had finally rolled around, which should have made him feel better.

How he loved seeing the lovelies out in their flimsy strappy tops, shorts/skirts and flip-flops.

It had been thirteen months since his mother had committed suicide – eight since he'd finally buried her remains on Porthcawl beach.

The sea has her now...

Huffing, he let his shoulders drop. "I need to get my life back on track," he said aloud. He looked around – the house, and everything in it, looked alien to him. "Maybe I should burn the place to the ground?"

'You can't spend any more of your time moping, sir!' Mr. Tickles said from somewhere behind him.

"I know..." he said, letting his words trail off. A large van stopped in his street, due to traffic build up. It was brightly-coloured by the Stars and Stripes – a huge bald eagle with curled talons could be seen on the door. Simone couldn't see the passenger or driver of the vehicle, as the windows were blacked out.

Written over the red, white and blue on the side of the van were the words *'Flesh Flaying Fiends: the world's most deranged dominatrix act'*. The sound of it made his balls ache. There was a mobile number listed below the words. Quickly, he grabbed his own phone and took the number down.

As the van pulled off, Simone rang the number. A woman with a thick, south American accent answered. "Hello, Flesh Flaying Fiends, Chrissy speaking – how can I help you?"

His breath hitched in his throat.

"Hello?!" she repeated with a sharper edge to her tone.

"Who the fuck is it?" he heard another woman ask in the background.

"I don't know, Coops – some douchebag heavy breather! *Hello*?!"

Simone ended the call by snapping his phone closed. The American lady went away. "Dom…i…na…trix…" By breaking the word up, it helped him to digest it. "Can't say I've ever heard it before. What does it mean, Mr. Tickles? Have you heard that word before?"

'*It probably means that they're a bunch of dirty whores that need a good whipping and fucking!*'

He didn't have the internet in his house or on his phone, as he wasn't interested in it, so he couldn't check the meaning. Nervously, he opened his phone and redialled the number.

"Hello?!" the same woman said, clearly pissed.

"Oh, uh, h-hey…" he stuttered.

"Yeah?"

"I…"

"Are you the same person that called about five minutes ago?!"

"Oh…Er…Yeah, it was me…"

"Why you wasting peoples' time, bro?!"

"I'm sorry...I didn't know what to say," he confessed.

"Look, what can—"

"What does dom...i...na..trix mean?" he blurted. This provoked a shriek-like laugh from the other end of the phone. He smiled. *I like her...* A giggle escaped him.

"Dominatrix? Well, that would be telling, big boy. What do you think it means?!"

He looked at Mr. Tickles, licked his lips, and took a deep breath before answering. "That you're a bunch of dirty whores that need a good whipping and fucking!"

'*Ad a boy, sir! Tell the little strumpets how it is!*'

More shrieks of laughter, followed by her covering the phone and talking to the other person in the van. He couldn't quite work out what they were saying, but he guessed that they were making fun of him. He liked it.

"Ha-ha, is that so?!" she asked.

Oh, boy, do I like her... After so many months of living in the shadows, staying on the cusp of society, it was nice to finally have some interaction. He was starting to remember what it was like to talk to people. To talk to nice women, especially pretty ones.

"Are you pretty, Chrissy?!" He couldn't believe he had asked her that. *Fuck it.* "Bet you have nice legs, too!"

"Oh, you're a cheeky one! Mama's going to have to put a collar and lead on you, *dog!*"

He had no idea what she meant, but he liked it. His cock pulsed and pushed against the front of his trousers. Grabbing his zip with his free hand, he lowered it and reached inside for his dick.

As she spoke, he rubbed it to the sound of her voice.

"I bet you like the sounds of that, don't you, beast?"

All he could do was groan.

19

"Are you fucking playing with yourself, you dirty fuck?!"

Her giggling pushed him over the edge – he couldn't hold his orgasm back. His hot load erupted out the end of his cock and shot up the curtains and splashed the drapes.

"*Ugh!*" he gasped to the sound of her giggles.

"My, you're an interesting one, cowboy. Why don't you come on down to the Klitty Kingdom tonight?"

"On the front?" His breathing came in ragged tears.

"Yeah. I'll *show* you what a dominatrix is."

"Okay…"

"The show starts at nine sharp. Make sure you're there. And when you've seen the show, make sure you come over and say hi!"

The line went dead, which was followed by a dreadful buzzing sound. He pulled his mobile from his ear and hung up.

"Nine, she said. Should I, Mr. Tickles?"

'*Affirmative, sir – you need to get back in the saddle, as they say. Besides, it would be nice to have some clunge around here! It's been far, far too long.*'

A broad smile appeared on Simone's face. The call had been the thing he'd needed to help get him out of the doldrums.

Simone could feel the clouds of misery finally starting to lift.

Attention – that's the thing he craved most.

At precisely eight fifteen, Simone was standing outside the shithole named the Klitty Kingdom – a flea-bitten, ramshackle dump known locally as the Fuck Pit. The structure looked as though it was being held together by bubblegum and jism; most of the paint and plaster had come away from the exterior walls. It was the type of place where you wiped your feet on the way out.

As he was about to put his hand on the door handle to open it, he noticed the lacklustre brass was coated in dried blood and snot. His stomach back flipped and eyes rolled like marbles.

"Dirty cunts." Carefully, he covered his hand with the cuff of his jacket and pulled the door outward – he was immediately hit by the smell of stale twat, cigarette smoke and suspect ale.

Releasing a held breath, Simone stepped inside and almost instantly regretted it – the place was rammed so full that he couldn't see the bar, let alone the stage. He'd never been very good at handling large crowds, but he was determined not to let that spoil his evening. *As if she's going to remember me after a brief conversation over the phone...I'm sure she's spoken to loads of guys today.* "Chrissy..." he said, letting the name roll off his tongue.

Lightly pushing past people to get to the bar, he excused himself as he went. When he finally got there, he realised he was standing next to a guy on a stool – he was slumped over the bar. A rank stench of shit and piss waved off him, bringing Simone to the conclusion that the guy had soiled himself in his intoxicated state.

"Devine," he muttered.

"Help you?!" asked the barman, who reminded Simone of a boxer, what with his flat nose, ravaged looks and missing teeth.

"Coke, please."

A few sniggers erupted from behind him, followed by "Sissy", "Faggot" and "Fairy". He didn't care what the fuck others thought of him – he wasn't an ale, cider or lager drinker. He preferred wine, and he certainly wasn't ordering something like that in a bar full of brawler types.

When the barman returned, he slammed a can of Coke down on the bar. "That'll be three quid, pal," he barked.

"Next time, wear a mask, Dick!" Simone uttered.

"Excuse me?!" the barman spat.

"I said, lovely." He handed the man his money and turned to leave. As he did, he looked down and noticed he'd been standing in a puddle of piss. "Delicious."

Moving on, Simone weaved, ducked and bobbed his way through the crowd until he was close to the stage. It wasn't as classy or clean as Bunnies, and lacked personality. The poles that the women used looked grubby.

Looking at his watch, he noticed it was almost five past nine.

Any minute now, surely...

As if the compare had heard him, he stepped from behind a pair of gaudy curtains at the back of the stage and addressed the crowd via the microphone he held in his fat hand. He seemed like just the kind of guy who would own/work a place such as the Klitty Kingdom – fat, sweaty, greasy-looking, and balding. No, not completely bald: He had a few strands of hair that acted as a comb over. His jacket, much like the shades he wore, looked as though it had stepped out of the seventies.

Do the curtains act as a Tardis... he mused?

"Ladies and gentlemen, boys and girls of all ages...Welcome to the Klitty Kingdom!"

People all around him started to whistle, howl, applaud and cheer. "Bring out the Yankee fanny!" someone yelled as the raucous died down.

"Be patient, you little cunt!" the compare joked. "Tonight, and every night for the next fortnight, we are proud to present to you the lovely ladies from across the Atlantic Ocean, the Flesh Flaying Fiends!" he growled down the microphone. "The usual ladies will be around to strip, dance and tease you into comas as usual…But first, the wild, wet and devious threesome that's guaranteed to put a stiffness in your drawers…"

The loudmouth stepped aside and put his arm out in a sweeping motion. The lights dimmed and out from behind the curtain stepped three of the most glamorous girls Simone had ever seen.

"Making up the Flesh Flaying Fiends are Chrissy Sandoval, Marianne Elsie and Christina Cooper!" the compare bellowed from the shadows.

Simone's thoughts were drowned out by wolf whistles – not that he could think of much. Before him, the women came out in a line, led by whom he took to be Chrissy, considering the order the announcer had reeled off.

She was rather tall for a woman, five seven or eight, with good legs and prominent hips and a striking waistline. *Her tits are small, but perky and juicy,* he thought as he watched her naked form sashay across the stage. *The voice definitely matches the body!*

Her skin wasn't blemished by tattoos or piercings. He anticipated her turning around so he could see her arse, which he knew would be a perfect peach. But before he managed to glimpse it, he caught sight of her hairless twat.

*Ohh…*He groaned and fought the urge to touch his cock, even though he knew some of the other guys around him were doing the same.

He didn't have time to keep looking at Chrissy, as his eyes were then drawn to the woman behind her.

Marianne wore nothing but a bandanna. In her left hand, she held an impressive bullwhip; in her right, she twirled a nightstick coiled in barbed wire.

"Fuck! That thing looks painful," he said, smiling.

Marianne appeared to be slightly taller, fuller bodied and bigger breasted than Chrissy. Unlike her Flesh Flaying sister, she had tattoos. One visible above her left breast was in the design of Medusa's head. Her snake hair stretched out far on both sides, with all the heads spitting venom. Their beady eyes glowed yellow, and stood out in the garish lighting inside the Kingdom.

As Marianne strutted her stuff, she cracked her whip with a fierce flick of her wrist, which made Simone's hard-on waver but remain. She looked like hell on legs, which made him ache with pure lust and pleasure.

Pre-jism leaked out of his cock and glued his pants to his bits.

Behind Marianne was Christina, or "Coops" as Simone had heard her being referred to earlier in the day by Chrissy. Unlike her sordid sisters, she wore one article of clothing – a pair of hot pants with a huge strap-on cock, which was black in colour and glistened under the light. On her head, she had a leather punk cap, which was trimmed with spiked studs and small chains. She had her pierced tongue poking out.

Coops was the smallest of the three by far, breast and stature-wise, but Simone found her spattering of freckles a real turn-on, and he was eager to see what she had planned with her strap-on.

Pyros kicked to life and heavy metal music erupted through the speakers dotted around the room – a band was singing about how the torture never stops. Then, the lights were killed and coloured spotlights burst into action, flooding the bar area, stage and girls in a psychedelic glow, giving them the appearance of something psychotic lurking in the shadows.

Sparks flashed.

Bangs and puffs of smoke startled the punters as they watched on in complete bemusement and excited curiosity.

Who are these amazing women? Simone thought, barely able to hear the voice inside his own head as the crazy train before him chuffed on. *Amazing. I've never heard, let alone seen, anything like this before.*

"Dom…i…na…trix…" he mouthed. "Is this it?!"

Over the course of the next fifteen minutes, Simone watched on in wide-eyed wonderment as the ladies did their thing on stage.

Finally, the music was cut and Marianne stepped out of the pyro fog and slanted coloured beams, all tit and attitude. She addressed all the "Maggots" before her. "Who out there's man enough to take the kind of punishment me and my Flesh Flaying sisters are able to dish out?"

Simone's jaw slackened – they were looking for volunteers to disgrace and humiliate.

Behind Marianne, he saw Coops thrust her massive strap-on as she dangled a small, steel contraption before her. It looked like some form of cage and appeared homemade…

Simone gulped, but shook with the horn. Before he could shoot his arm skyward in a shrinking crowd, another beat him to it.

"Pick me!" the eager man bellowed. Looking over the audience, which seemed to breathe with relief, Simone saw a skinny arm sticking up – it looked as though someone's head had grown a limb. "Me, please!" the person continued, shoving his way to the front.

The tallish man with a shaved head rushed up the stage steps. He wore black leather trousers and a t-shirt that bore the words 'I love it in every hole' on its back. "Looks like we have a brave dog, girls!" Marianne said into the microphone. Behind her, Simone could see Coops and Chrissy laughing. "What's your name, beast?!" she asked him, then thrust the microphone in his face.

"Chris," he said. His voice sounded shaky.

Marianne, who was roughly the same height as her participant, turned the man around to face the crowd, who cheered.

On the front of his t-shirt, he had a huge, circumcised cock – the bell-end was pierced.

"Chris Hall!" Simone blurted. "Shit, I was in school with that fucker," he said to himself. "Give it to the bastard!"

"Strip, worm!" Marianne ordered him.

"Hey?! I thought I was going to get a lap—"

"Strip!" Marianne yelled, then struck her prey across the face with her barbed nightstick.

Chris went to ground and clutched his torn cheek. He cried in agony, but then gasped in shock as Coops and Chrissy ripped at his clothes. Within seconds, he was naked. Stocks were then rolled onto stage, and he was locked into them.

When Simone didn't think things could get any stranger, or exciting, Chris was tortured, beaten, fucked and humiliated to within an inch of his life – they pulverized his cock and balls before locking his bits into the homemade cage. As Marianne whipped him with her bullwhip, which took more than a pound of skin, Coops raped him with her strap-on.

Before he could start screaming, a ball with a couple of straps attached to it was rammed into his open gob – the belts fastened behind his head.

Some of the onlookers had walked out at this point. Others had thrown their guts up.

But not Simone – he was enthralled. It fed his devious side.

He wanted to know and experience more.

By the time Coops was finished pounding Chris' arse, the anus-busting wang was covered in shit and blood, and a pool of piss had spread out around the stocks that homed the humiliated man.

After an hour of punishment at the hands of the Flesh Flaying Fiends, Chris' eyes were rolling around inside his head and his knees were knocking. When they finally released him, he collapsed to the floor and rolled into his own urine. His body was spent, ruined and weeping red from multiple wounds.

His loose anus, which must have felt like he'd shit a rocket, emitted one fart after the other – it sounded like staggered machine-gun fire to Simone.

They totally dominated him! Then it finally clicked – "Dom...i...na...trix!"

"Any other brave—"

Before Marianne could finish her sentence, Simone put his hand high – his balls were that tight with excitement, he feared they would rupture in his pants.

"Get up here, *maggot!*" her voice boomed. "What's you name, your pathetic piece of shit?!"

"Simone," he said, his voice but a whisper.

"He has a girl's name!" Coops said.

"That's the fucker who kept ringing earlier!" Chrissy pointed out.

"Oh, so you're our heavy breather!" Marianne said. "Ladies, help him with his clothes."

As Simone was stripped, stagehands rolled Chris to the end of the stage and pushed him off. His body hit the floor with a dull thud. His clothes were thrown after him.

"What a little cock!" Coops said, pulling a crop from behind her back. She lashed his hardness repeatedly before ordering him into the stocks.

Her whipping had hurt at first – so too had the butt fucking – but he'd thoroughly enjoyed it, and he found he was able to take everything they gave him, much to Chrissy's obvious joy, as she'd masturbated in front of him.

After they finally broke him, he too was thrown off stage, just like Chris. He found he couldn't move – his legs didn't work and his body felt like jelly. Pain exuberated through him, which he welcomed. At some point, he slipped into unconsciousness and woke to find most people had left the club.

Rolling onto his side, he managed to get to all fours and crawled to a nearby chair with his clothes in tow.

"Hi," he heard someone say.

When he got to the chair, he found it hard in pulling himself up and sitting on it – he winced when he planted himself down.

"You okay there, cowboy?"

He knew the voice. Through squinted, tear-filled eyes, he looked about him and saw Chrissy sitting on a chair close by. She was fully clothed, much to his disappointment.

"You must have blacked out. The club's been closed for almost an hour," she said, smiling.

"Wha…wha…" he tried, but the words wouldn't come.

"You're quite the punch bag, sugar – you have a dom at home?"

"Water…" he gasped.

"Can we get a water over here, please?"

"Sure!" someone called back at Chrissy.

"Another beer, too," she asked.

"Coming up."

Simone snuck another glance at her – her legs looked very long, and shiny.

"You like my yams, sailor?"

"I don't have a…dom," he confessed. "This was my first time."

"You play the game like an expert, Simone. That is your name, right?"

He nodded. "Yeah. I think one of my ribs might be broken…"

"Nah, you're just bruised." Her beer was plonked in front of her. "Thanks."

"Here," the barman said, slamming his water down on the table.

Simone looked at the discoloured water, which had bits floating around in it, and thanked the man. He took a hearty swallow before replacing the glass on the table. "That's fucking disgusting!" he said.

She giggled. "I like you!"

"Why are you still here? More to the point, why am I?!"

"I told them to leave you here."

"Why?"

"Because I wanted to take you back to my hotel room, sweetie," she said.

***

"Son, are you okay?!" the priest asked.

"Huh?!" Simone said, coming out of his thoughts.

"Are you okay?!"

"Oh, er…Yes. Sorry. I…"

"I thought something was wrong…"

"No, Father. Sorry," he said, giving the note he held in his hand a shake. "I was just about to start reading." But before he did, he replied to Chrissy's message.

"Okay."

"*Dear Simone, by the time you read this, I'll be gone. I'm sorry, baby boy, I just couldn't keep going the way we were – I've ruined the special bond between a mother and son, and I blame myself for the man you have become. One day, I hope you can find it in your heart to forgive me for everything I have put you through. I cling to the hope that we will meet again, in a place where we can be together forever. All my love, Mam. XXXX,*" Simone said, wiping a tear from his eye. He managed to keep himself together as he held Mr. Tickles close to his chest – he hugged his toy clown as fiercely as he could.

"I'm sorry to hear that, my child. What did she mean by ruining the special bond between mother and child?"

He didn't really want to answer the priest's question. After all, he hadn't told anyone what really went on between him and his mother. Not even Her. *But isn't that why I came here? To finally get* everything *off my chest before I…*

"We were intimate, Father."

"You and *your* mother?!"

"Yes."

"Oh..." he gasped.

'I don't know why the fuck he's sounding so fucking appalled by your actions, sir – he probably touches the choir boys on the quiet!' Mr. Tickles said, smiling.

"I know how it must sound, Father..."

"My poor child."

"I can't say anything. After all, I did enjoy it – maybe I encouraged it more than I should have..."

"You can't blame yourself – she was the adult and should have known better. You poor lamb."

"She never allowed me to enter her body – we only played and bathed together, Father. I think she took her life before it got to that stage."

"What stage?"

"Sex. I think she may have been worried that's where the relationship was heading. I hate her for taking that from me, too. I loved her, Father. I loved her more than a son should love his mother, but I couldn't help it."

"Oh, my..."

"Will there be forgiveness for me, Father? Will I be allowed to enter into the Kingdom of Heaven – to walk through the pearly-white gates? Will I indeed meet my mother along with my maker? Please tell me! I need to know."

"Yes, my boy. As I told you earlier, our Lord is most forgiving of the sins his lambs commit. He died for them, after all."

"And my mother—will she be waiting for me?"

"Yes. Even your mother's sins will be forgiven. Her soul cleansed."

"It wasn't just my mother's fault, Father. Other women have helped push me down the wrong path."

"I see. Go on."

As if on cue, his mobile rumbled. Opening it, he saw it was Chrissy – she'd responded to his reply.

"There was once this American woman…"

***

After she finished her beer and he drained the last of his dirty water, she led him out of the Klitty Kingdom and to the streets beyond, which were dead quiet – not even a car drove by as they walked and talked. The only sound came from the crashing waves as they smashed against the rocks.

"What time is it?" he asked. "My watch was broken earlier…"

"Just past one A.M," she said.

"Where are you taking me?"

"I told you, back to my hotel room."

"Where are you staying? Is it the Seabank Hotel?"

"Yes, how did you know that?!"

"It's the most popular…Are your friends staying there, too?"

"Look, let's cut the small talk – are you telling me you've never been whipped and beaten by a woman before? That was your first time?"

He nodded coyly. "Is it shameful that I enjoyed it?"

She smiled at him. "Come on!" she said, then led him down to the sands.

"Hey, where—"

"Come on!" she said, pulling him by his hand.

When she got him on the beach, she found them a secluded spot and started to strip.

"Leave your tights on..." he said nervously.

"Ooh, does daddy like them?" she asked, strutting around in her panties, bra and tights – the rest of her clothes had been discarded. Thrown to the sands with gay abandon. As she did a little dance for him, she rubbed her thighs and blew him kisses.

All he could do was stand there and watch her. *I must look like a cardboard cut out! Do something. Touch her,* his mind screamed. *She clearly wants you to.*

"You can't be shy, not after what you endured tonight – all the girls laughing at you! The crowd, too."

He shook his head. Slowly, he put one foot in front of the other, as though he was learning to walk for the first time – his legs were stiff. Simone felt like a reanimated corpse.

"Come on, baby!" she purred.

He halted and looked at her. He couldn't stop the words from tumbling out of his mouth – "I've never been with a woman!"

Sure, Sian and he had done things together, but that was a long time ago – he'd forgotten most of it. Besides, a fully grown, developed woman had never fucked him.

Chrissy stopped dancing and looked at him. Her smile faded.

"A woman has never touched me," he said. The thought that he was lying made him feel as though he was betraying his mother's memory. *Fuck her, she left me.* "I've been lonely...I have no one!"

Then, unexpectedly, tears raced down his cheeks.

"Hey, come on, it's okay!" she said, stepping closer to him and taking him by the hand. "You want to tell Chrissy what's wrong?"

No, I can't tell anyone what's wrong, especially a woman I've only known for five minutes, he thought.

"I'm nineteen years old, and I've never been with a lady!"

"Sh!" she said, putting her arms around him.

He collapsed against her body and placed his head against her chest.

She smells like Mam…

The feel of her legs against his instantly turned him on – his hardness pushed against her thigh.

"Touch me!" she whispered down his ear.

"I…"

She took his hands in hers, and put them on her arse. "Go on, feel it…"

As she nibbled his neck, he caressed her arse and kissed her – it wasn't long before they were both naked and rolling around in the sand. When she had him underneath her, she rode his cock to the tune of multiple orgasms as he fumbled with her petite tits and teased her nipples.

When they were both spent, Chrissy collapsed onto his chest. It didn't take her long to drift off to sleep, leaving him to drink in what had happened. It was the first time he had been happy in almost a year.

He may have still been broken at that point, but she had certainly helped in putting him back together.

Maybe I do have a chance at living a normal life now? he thought, looking up at the dark sky, which was star and moonless. Looking down at Chrissy, who snored lightly, he wondered how different things could be if he found himself a nice girl like her. *Maybe she'll be my girl? I'm sure Mr. Tickles and the gang will love her.*

With that happy thought in mind, Simone closed his eyes and tried to drift off to sleep by listening to the waves roll and then collide against the rocks.

He awoke to the sound of gulls screaming. After clearing the sand of sleep from the corners of his eyes, Simone noticed Chrissy was nowhere to be seen.

Did I dream it?! No, that's impossible.

Slowly, he sat up and looked all around him – the only thing he could see were seagulls fighting over food and early morning fishermen casting lines. The sun was barely up.

"Chrissy?" he called, his throat bone dry. *I knew it was too good to be true.*

As his head dropped, he noticed something odd about the sand in front of him. Getting up, he took a closer look. Someone had scrawled something in it.

"Come to the Klitty Kingdom tonight! I'll be waiting for you... Chrissy. Kisses," he read aloud. A smile spread across his face. "So, she does like me!"

After kicking the sand message away, he ran up the beach and didn't stop until he got home.

By the time eight o'clock rolled around, Simone was about ready to climb the walls in frustration. The day had been spent pacing the floorboards of his house, looking out the upper and lower windows of the house, cleaning and doing anything else he could think of to waste time.

"I can't wait to see her again, Mr. Tickles. I think she could be the one, you know."

'*Sir, just be careful. I don't want to see you hurt again. Not after mother...*'

"No, I'll be fine. It's not like she's going to walk out on me. She wants me!"

'*I'm sure you know what you're doing, sir. Do you plan to bring her back here tonight?*'

"Yes, if she'll come. We might end up spending the night on the beach again!"

'*Okay, sir. Just in case, I'll make sure myself and the rest of the Krulls are out of the way.*'

"Very good, Mr. Tickles. I'm going to head off soon, so if you can keep an eye on things around here, I'll be most grateful."

'*Affirmative, sir – you have nothing to worry about with me at the helm.*'

"I know the place is in good hands. I'll hopefully see you later – I would like to bring her back here."

'*Sir?*'

"Yes?"

'*I take it you know what dominatrix means now?*' Mr. Tickles asked, smiling.

Simone smiled back, remembering the lashings Marianne had given him with her whip, along with the clamps Coops had used to crush his nuts – the thought of it got him turned on.

"Oh, yes! You could say I do, Mr. Tickles. They had this little cage with them – Chrissy called it a male chastity device – and they locked my cock up in it and I couldn't get it fully stiff. The bars restricted it. It was amazing."

'*It sounds it. Maybe she'll do some kinky shit to you here tonight, sir. It sure would give me and the boys a few needed thrills.*'

"I'll see what I can do! Do you want me to put the TV on for you?"

'*Please, sir.*'

"Okay. I need to get the hell out of here – time is moving on!" Once he'd switched the TV on, Simone left Mr. Tickles to it. "See you later!" he called, closing the front door behind him.

By the time he got to the Klitty Kingdom, the show had already started. He cursed himself for having left the house so late, but his bad mood soon turned to happiness when he saw the Flesh Flaying Fiends working their magic up on stage.

As Marianne, who was dressed in all leather, ordered a male member of the audience to strip, her girls worked the poles behind her. Both Chrissy and Coops were dressed as schoolgirls – they wore pigtails, pleated skirts, knee-high socks and flimsy white shirts with loosened ties.

It was a marvel to watch.

When Chrissy spotted Simone in the crowd, she was upside-down on her pole with her skirt pulled back, revealing her pussy. She gave him a smile and a wave, which coaxed him to do the same. Some of the men in the audience turned to look at him with distaste.

He couldn't take his eyes off her. She was amazing, just like her smile.

When Marianne screamed at the 'maggot' at her feet, Simone looked at her – the poor bastard she had up on stage was now fitted with a collar and lead. She led him around like a dog before forcing him to take a shit and piss in front of everyone. When he whimpered he couldn't go, she kicked him in the nuts. Marianne continued to do this until the man finally pushed his waste out.

His humiliation seemed to go on and on, from having his nose rubbed in his own filth by Coops to licking the soles of Chrissy's high-heels.

Simone had never felt so turned on.

He knew he got off on shame at the hands of a woman, but he never thought he would have been turned on by being pushed around by one. To be beaten. This show had opened his mind – had broadened his horizon.

After the Flesh Flaying Fiends had finished with their latest victim, they wanted another. Immediately Simone put his hand in the air, but he was refused. He felt cheated as another male was picked from the crowd.

Turning his back on the show, Simone pushed his way to the bar, not watching where he was going.

"Hey, you fucking retard!" someone yelled at him. A rough hand grabbed his shoulder, and Simone was turned around to face a man roughly the same size as himself. "You made me spill my fucking drink!" he spat in Simone's face. His breath reeked of rum.

"Sorry, I'll buy you another…" Simone said, not looking for trouble. It had been a long time since he'd raised his hands in anger with another man.

Cartwright had been the last…

"Oh, is that so!" the man said, giving Simone a push. "How about a fucking sorry first, you little cunt!"

"I did apologise," Simone bit back. "Are you fucking deaf?" he continued, feeling his patience wane.

"You wha'?!" the man said, screwing his face up as though he couldn't understand what had been said to him. "Are you taking the piss out of me?!" He gave Simone another push.

He fell against a table, causing all the bottles and glasses that stood on it to rattle – contents were spilled.

"Hey, fucking watch it!" someone bellowed.

All the while, Simone could hear the Fiends doing their thing on stage, whilst he had some dickhead threatening him over something meaningless.

Before he knew it, his hand had wrapped around the neck of a beer bottle.

"Well?!" the man barked at Simone.

Without a second's hesitation, Simone brought the bottle up and cracked it across his attacker's face.

"*Argh!* My fucking eyes!" he said, clutching his face.

He wanted to plunge the ruined bottle into the guy's neck, but he managed to get a leash on his rage. *No, that would be stupid. Too many eyes.* He dropped his weapon and instead grabbed the man by his ears and pulled his head down swiftly. Simone brought his knee up to meet the guy's nose, which flattened like a ripe tomato.

The sound of bone crunching against his joint was beyond satisfying – within that moment, Simone could see why the girls on stage got a kick out of hurting people. It was exhilarating.

As his prey hit the deck, Simone dove on him and delivered lefts and rights to his wrecked face.

"I said I was fucking sorry!" he yelled as he punched and punched the man. "Maybe you'll fucking listen…"

Suddenly, Simone felt two sets of large hands on his arms.

"That's enough, sunshine!" someone said.

"He's had enough, and you're out of here!" said a second person.

"Wait, no! Chrissy!" Simone yelled.

"We don't want any more trouble!" the second voice said.

Someone punched Simone hard in his kidney, causing his breath to catch in his throat. He was led out the back of the club, where a pair of double doors were opened.

"One…Two…Three!" his escorts said as they threw him out into the alley.

His body crashed against a dozens bins. A cat pounced onto his stomach before scampering off into the night.

"Ugh!" Simone said, rolling onto his side.

"And fucking stay out!" one of them said to him.

"Yeah, we catch you back here again, we'll kick your arse, pal!" the other said.

Opening his eyes, Simone saw the two for the first time – they were huge. It was as if someone had stuffed a pair of gorillas into ill-fitting dinner suits.

He said nothing, just lay there and accepted his fate. "Chrissy…" he mouthed, holding his ribs.

Groaning, he got to his feet and dusted himself down – a banana skin and other bits of rubbish had clung to his shirt and jeans. "Ugh, fucking disgusting."

Undeterred by the thug-like bouncers, Simone stayed in the lane and waited for the girls to finish their show in the hope that Chrissy would come outside and look for him.

After a few hours passed, however, he was on the verge of surrender.

"She ain't coming!" he said to himself, sitting among the scattered bins. Rats scurried about him, but he didn't care.

Getting up to leave, he was stopped by the same doors he'd been thrown through opening at his back.

"Simone?" he heard a female voice whisper.

"Chrissy?!" he said into the gloom.

The next thing he heard was her high-heels clacking along the stone floor.

"Aw, I'm sorry," she said, throwing her arms around him. "Are you okay? They didn't hurt you, did they?"

"No," he said. The pain in his side had long since subsided. "Why didn't you allow me up on stage? Had you, I probably wouldn't have got attacked by that fucking bozo!"

She lowered her head to look at her feet – she still wore her schoolgirl outfit. "Sorry about that, too. It was my fault Marianne didn't pick you…"

"Why?!" he said, stepping out of the shadows to loom over her.

"Is that fucking shitbag bothering you, love?!" one of the gorillas asked from the doorway.

"Piss off!" Simone yelled back.

"You little fucking—"

"No, stop. It's okay. He's my friend," Chrissy told the bouncer.

"Are you sure about that?" Simone asked her.

"Yes, silly!" she said, smiling. "Want to take me home?!"

He saw that sparkle in her eye again – the same one he had seen last night. Her smile was beyond sexy. It was cheeky.

That night, they made love until the early hours. In the morning, before he had awoken, she had gone, just like she had done on the beach. A note had been left in his kitchen.

"Pick me up from the Klitty Kingdom tonight – I'll come back to yours…" he read.

For the following fortnight, that's pretty much how it went down between Simone and Chrissy: He would pick her up from work, take her home to fuck, and she would be gone by the next day.

Some nights, on his request, she would dominate him – spank him, tease him, dress him like a girl. Anything he wanted, she was only too glad to participate. She confessed to really liking him and wanting him to go back to the States with her.

"I can't, Chrissy. As much as I would love to," he'd told her.

"Why not? You could sell this house…Come with me! We could build a life together in America. You have nothing keeping you here."

"I'll think about it," had been his answer to an opportunity of a lifetime. To a woman he could see himself being truly happy with. Deep down, he had hoped she would stay to be with him…

And, on her last night in Wales, he thought she was going to tell him just that – that she was going nowhere. That the act would have to find a replacement. But no. Just like that, she had walked out of his life. Before going, she had taken his number and had promised to get in touch if she was in his neck of the woods ever again.

"You have my contact information: e-mail and both telephone numbers – home and mobile. If you change your mind about coming to the States, contact me. I'd love to have you over."

When she'd kissed him goodbye, he'd made a promise to himself – *I'll never wash my lips again.*

The night she left, Simone dwindled back into his black hole of depression. Thoughts of his mother returned to haunt him, making him think he was destined to be miserable for the rest of his life.

"You were right, Mr. Tickles – I should have watched myself. I've been let down by another woman. First my mother, and now Chrissy…"

***

"Do you also blame this woman you speak of for your ways, child?!"

"Until we started talking, Father, no, I didn't. But now, the more I think about it, yes, I do."

"Why, my son? She presented you with an opportunity – you could have taken it. You could have avoided the sin you were to commit, had you left with her."

"You're right, but I couldn't. I just could not leave here, Father. Porthcawl is my home. It's where my mother brought me up. And, as much as I hated my mother for leaving me, I just wasn't ready to move on."

"Yet you expected her to drop everything and stay with you?"

"I thought you weren't supposed to judge, Father?!" Simone said with a harshness to his tone.

"Sorry if it sounded unsympathetic, my boy, but you have to see it from her side too."

Simone sighed. "I don't just blame her for leaving me, Father."

"Oh?"

"If it weren't for meeting her, then I would never have met Chaos. The woman who finally tipped me over the edge."

"Chaos?!"

"Yes, it was her dominatrix name."

"Oh, yes. I see. And how was Chrissy to blame for you meeting this, this Chaos person?"

"She'd given me a taste of the dominatrix ways. I wanted it. And as I sat at home, crippled by depression once more, it started to dwell on my mind. Not just the sex, but the punishment she had given me. I started to crave it, and so I went looking for it."

"I see. Go on."

"At first, I took it as a good sign. I mean, it got me out of the house – something which I hadn't done since Chrissy had left a couple of months prior. I was meeting people, going to clubs...I felt great. I felt alive once more, Father."

"Hmm, I see. And was it in one of these clubs that you met Chaos?"

"Yes. It was in a club in Cardiff. You see, these types of places can only be found in the city; here in Porthcawl, a place like that could never thrive. Bunnies, the place where my mother used to work, closed down due to lack of interest, which was a shame. It was a safe haven of mine."

"Did you immediately find this Chaos character, my child?!"

"Oh no, Father...It took a lot of searching, and a lot of acceptable mistakes, until I found her..."

***

When you're into the depraved, it's hard to find a place to play. A clean, healthy and decent place. A place where you feel safe. Simone hadn't been outside of Porthcawl much, and so city life, fun and games were new to him.

But that's where he needed to be if he was ever going to get his new kind of jollies.

He would never have thought of going to Cardiff had he not heard the whispers on the streets of Porthcawl: during off-season, a seaside town can be one of the murkiest places on the planet. One Saturday night, whilst trying to score a bit of debauched kink, Simone had overheard a couple of fairground hands talking about the seedier side of Cardiff city. About how a bloke can get "any kind of fuck" he wanted. About how the "boys like to dress as women" and how the "men like to get whipped and have big black dicks stuffed up their arses." About how you can "pay to sniff cocaine out of the arse-crack of stripper." And about how a few dodgy alleys in the middle of the city were home to such places for perverts, freaks and weirdos.

The city was the place to play.

The rich kids knew it.

The businessmen knew it.

And, after eavesdropping, Simone knew it...

At the time, he had wondered if he would find dominatrix fun in the city, on top of everything else he had heard.

He'd planned to find out, and so, that very next weekend, he'd hit the streets of Cardiff.

Getting off the train at ten P.M in the city felt strange. As he stood among a scant amount of people on the platform, he couldn't help but feel like a rabbit caught in headlights.

Simone had to admit, he was scared.

He'd heard lots of horror stories about the city – the crime, the violence.

I wish Mr. Tickles was with me, he thought. *Come on, I'll be fine. It's not like I can't take care of myself.*

Before he exited the train station, Simone removed his wallet from his back pocket and stored it in the breast pocket of his jacket, along with his train ticket.

Even though the night had settled in, the city was bustling, as though it was the middle of the day. The neon lights lit his way as he went in search for something beyond explicit.

Would he find it?

He didn't know, but he was sure as hell going to try.

Firstly, he decided to hit a few pubs to help loosen himself up. Not only that, he thought he may catch people talking about 'parties' going on at certain clubs around the city.

When that failed, Simone decided to keep moving. To keep searching and checking out all the different pubs and clubs he came across.

After an hour or so of being on the street, he finally came across a place he thought he might be in luck with.

The name of the joint, which was lit up in pink, gaudy lettering, told him all he thought he would need to know: *Leather and Ice.*

"Sounds just like what I'm looking for!" he said aloud. As he was about to enter, someone from behind called him a "Shit-shoveller". Simone thought nothing of it and continued to make his entrance.

Once through one set of double saloon doors, he found another set – beyond the frosted glass, he could see coloured disco lights flashing. They kept in sync with the heavy thud of cheesy nightclub music.

Ugh! Not my type of music by a far cry! he thought. *Still, I might find the exact kind of person I'm looking for.* Taking a quick look down at himself, Simone smoothed his shirt, ran a hand through his thick black hair, and walked through the next set of doors with bated breath.

"Here goes nothing!" he said, exhaling.

As he walked through the doors, the disco music cut, and on came "Legs" by ZZ Top, which Simone found to be pretty apt – the sight before him was breathtaking. The dance and bar area crawled with women. Not a man, other than himself, was in sight.

There were legs on display everywhere.

Most of the women wore tiny, ridiculously short skirts with either heels or boots. Some wore corsets; other wore just bras or flimsy see-through tops. Erect nipples were illuminated by the flashy-flicky-coloured lights that were both headache inducing and luring to the spectacle before him.

Above, women danced in steel cages suspended from the ceiling.

Waiters, who appeared to be the only men in sight, worked in nothing but black trousers, shoes and dickie bows – they wore cuffs, but no shirts. Their bodies rippled with muscle and shone with sleek sheens.

Even though there were multiple barmen, they all appeared to be the same, as though there was a conveyor belt somewhere spitting them out of a backroom acting as a warehouse. With their matching attire and stature, they all had luscious black hair, blue eyes which screamed *take me to bed*, and smiles that could melt the hardest of hearts.

But it wasn't the boys he was interested in, even though he found their role fascinating, and was certainly a job vacancy he could fill – it was the women and their legs he wanted.

He'd always been a leg man. Tits and arse were nice, but not as good as a cracking set of pins. Of course, the thigh had to be just right. In his mind, the perfect thighs were ones that were slightly thicker.

Oh, how they look good in tights.

And, as he roamed among the cougars, tarts and teens, Simone sought out his thick-thighed lady – maybe he would find one with a panache for whipping and beating men with a bamboo shoot, whip, crop or anything else that came to hand.

Cheekily, he whipped a large glass of wine off a tray a waiter was carrying and kept walking, much to the squeaky protest at his back.

Sue me, dickhead! he thought, taking a large gulp of red and smiling.

As a scantily clad female passed him, he grabbed a handful of her arse cheek and kept moving.

Her little yelp of shock, possibly pleasure, caused a current of excitement to jolt his cock awake – not that it was in that much of a slumber. Not with the amount of pins on display.

Hot pants, stockings, tights, short-shorts, French knickers, g-strings...It was endless.

And the boots they are wearing!

Simone had seen a lot of different attire for women, having grown up around strippers, but some of the things on display here were new to him.

Some of the lovelies wore boots that went right up their thighs.

Breathtaking!

When "Legs" came to an end, a song Simone didn't know came over the speakers, but it had a hard edge to it.

I hope they keep these kinds of song choices up! he thought, moving through the crowd and allowing his hand to grab and caress buttock and thigh alike.

A few of the women gave him black looks; others squealed in delight. The odd one or two spat something at him, but he didn't care – he felt like a lion parading through his jungle. They were his playthings, whether they liked it or not.

Fucking whores.

Smiling, he took another sip of wine.

Then, he stepped into a clearing – at the back of the club was a seating area. It was cordoned off by velvet cords and signs that read "VIP Lounge." As he was about to turn to walk back the way he had come, a voice chirped, "A *man!*"

"Huh?!" Simone said, turning back.

"*Ooo!* An outsider. Love it. How dangerous of you, babe!" the cougar said.   At a guess, he would have pegged her to be in her fifties, but she had the prettiest face he had ever seen. Her accent wasn't local, either.

"Dangerous?!" Simone said. He wondered if he looked as stupid as he sounded.

"And such attire! Oh, you're just divine. A damp patch waiting to happen!" she said.

"Are you talking to me?!" Simone asked, pointing a finger at his chest.

"Why, yes, you silly thing. Come, take a seat next to Francesca."

"It says it's a VIP area, er…Fran…"

"Cesca, my dear. And do ignore that – I'm a regular. I do as I please. Come!" she said, patting the spare sofa cushion at her side. "I won't bite!"

Yeah? You may get somewhere with me if you do, you fucking stinker!

He felt a smile crease his face as he watched her pull her very short skirt up that little bit further. *Any more, and I'll be able to see your furry cup!*

Stepping across the room, he loomed over her – her legs looked amazing beneath the black stockings she wore. As she crossed her leg over the other, he noticed she was wearing suspenders, heels and a garter.

At her side, he spotted a crop and leather mask with a zipper for a mouth.

On seeing the crop, he couldn't believe his luck.

She wore very little make-up, which caused her beautiful brown eyes to stand out, along with her high cheekbones. Her hands were gloved in lace and her torso was tied into a corset, which enhanced her very small tits.

He could tell she was excited, as her nipples were poking through the fabric that encased them.

"Rather delicious, aren't you!" Simone confessed.

"My, what a big handsome charmer you are!" She giggled. "Please, sit."

"Thank you," Simone said, saddling up next to her. She was much smaller than he'd first thought, now he was sat at her side.

"Would you like another wine?" she asked, spying his near-empty glass.

"Please." Swallowing the dregs, he put the glass on a table in front of him.

"Excuse me!" Francesca called one of the Adonis-like waiters.

"Yes, ma'am?" he said, giving Simone a funny look.

What's his fucking problem? he thought.

"Another G&T for me and a large glass of the house's finest red, please," she said. Her tone was smooth. Silk-like.

Her exposed thighs kept catching Simone's eyes – he couldn't help but snatch looks here and there.

"Are you drawn to them, dear?" she asked him, rucking her skirt up that little bit more.

"Oh, I'm sorry...I didn't mean to stare..."

"No, that's quite all right. Would you like to touch?"

He nodded, but not in an eager way.

She smiled. "What's your name?"

"Simone."

"Oo, how exotic. Isn't that Italian for Simon?"

"Yes," he said, nodding and smiling.

"What's so funny?" she asked, a smile spreading across her face.

"Nothing. Well, not really."

"Go on, don't be coy."

Before Simone could answer, the waiter butted in with their drinks.

"Leave them on the table," she said, not taking her eyes off Simone. "Start me a tab."

"Sure," the waiter said, turning to leave.

Simone gave him a quick look. *There's that fucking look again – what is his problem?* Simone saw a smirk develop on the waiter's cocky-looking mug.

"Why does he keep looking at me as though I'm an alien?!"

Now it was Francesca's turn to giggle. "They don't tend to like out-of-towners in here, sweetie. Don't sweat it."

Then he put his hand on her thigh. "Better?" he asked.

"Mm, much."

"What's the mask for?"

"My gimp," she said.

"What's a gimp?"

She smiled. "Let's just say it's a man that I keep under control..."

"Where is he?!"

"I haven't found him. Yet!" she said, looking at Simone. She looked hungry, but not for food.

"Will you whip me? Make me parade around like a girl? Put a collar and lead on me?"

"Wow! Steady on! You're making me hot!" she admitted. His hand crept up her thigh. "You have the Midas touch!"

He watched in wide-eye wonder as her bottom lip trembled. Her teeth could be heard chattering.

These fucking legs! he thought. *Amazing.* They were the right side of chunky – not too fat and not too skinny.

"How would you like to worship them?"

His hand retracted as he looked at her. "What do you mean?"

"Well, my little deviant Simone, how would you like to play with them until you heart was content, but only if you were good to your mistress?"

"A mistress as in a dominatrix?"

She giggled, then smiled. "Yes."

"Please!" he said, which almost sounded like a beg.

She had him hooked, causing him to keep moving his hand closer to her crotch. By the time he discovered she had a cock and was indeed a man dressed as a woman with tits, he didn't care.

His dick was leaking come into his pants – he was practically panting. His ache was great. His hand curled around her fat, stubby hardness. His hand slid up and down her shaft...

Before leaving the sofa and club, they both came. Twice.

That night, Simone left Leather and Ice with Francesca, and a new friendship blossomed.

Over the course of the three months they were 'friends', Francesca taught Simone many things about the underground sex scene he so craved to be a part of. After he told her about the Flesh Flaying Fiends and his relationship with Chrissy, and how he longed for a dominatrix in his life, she told him it wasn't as "simple as that."

That you didn't just *get* a dominatrix.

That you had to get to know the person.

That trust needed to be built up between the dom and sub.

As she taught him the ways, how and what clubs to visit and not, Francesca allowed him to worship her legs for the three months they stayed in each other's company.

It was during this relationship that Simone learned more about the usage of a cock cage, and the relationship between the wearer of the chastity device and the 'key holder', which was very straightforward, really.

When the man/slave agreed to surrender himself to his mistress/dom, his cock and balls were then locked away so he couldn't fuck or touch it – unless his key keeper allowed it, of course.

Francesca was a good mistress, but that was only because Simone was such a good slave – he looked after her legs as though they were his own. He'd wash them, shave them, cream them, dress them...

The best part for Francesca? She didn't need to satisfy him. He was happy to have his cock locked away as long as he got to play with her legs.

However, after three months, she got bored.

She was bored by the fact that Simone never wanted to fuck, suck or pleasure her arsehole in some way.

And so she called it off, leaving Simone heartbroken once again.

Although he'd had his heart and head fucked with once more, Simone refused to go back to the person he had been: the recluse.

This time, Simone pushed on with his life.

Did it matter women kept letting him down?

There was a whole world of them out there – he just had to find the right one.

Not long after his relationship with Francesca ended, Simone struck up a new friendship with another she-male named Porsche.

Like Simone, she too was new to the underground sex scene, and was very much an interesting character.

After meeting in a club by the name of Whips and Chains, which was buried down a side street out of harm's way, Simone came to learn very quickly what Porsche was all about.

Unlike Francesca, Porsche liked to be kept as a sissy slave – to be dressed up all pretty in stockings and ribbons. She existed for one reason and one reason only: to suck dick and please her master in any way he wanted.

She wasn't interested in being pleasured, and so kept her cock and balls in a cage – the padlock had been glued in place, so it was never coming off. Porsche had once been married, but her wife had left when he'd decided to go full transsexual.

"She couldn't put up with me taking boys back to the house, Simone. She hated what I was. What I couldn't control," Porsche had confided in him one evening whilst she was drinking.

Porsche had also told Simone that he had killed his wife and buried her in their garden, but Simone had discarded that, taking it as being the ravings of a bitter drunk.

He'd allowed her to pleasure him, just like he'd had fun and games with Francesca – Simone always took himself as a red-blooded male that loved nothing more than pussy, tits and arse, but since entering into the depraved, he found he was liking all sorts of fun and games.

Besides, he'd argued with himself, *they are womanly. They have breasts, slinky bodies, and pretty faces. And, I never let Francesca fuck me. I'll never allow Porsche too, either. That's never going to happen. I'm not a complete fucking poof.*

Truth be told, Simone was in his element.

At this point, he wasn't sure what he was looking for.

And then it happened.

After a few months of good times with Porsche, Simone moved on after meeting and falling in love with a woman by the name of Charlotte Ros, or Chaos, as he later found out.

***

"You see, Father, when Chaos came along, I thought all my worries were finally over. I thought I'd found my perfect dream woman. Even though I was having fun at this point, and Porsche and Francesca had pulled me out of my despondency, I still felt as though I was missing something. That a part of my jigsaw was amiss.

"Yes, my son. And was Chaos not what you were hoping her to be? Did she too let you down?"

Before he could answer, his phone bleeped. He removed it from his pocket – it was Chrissy. *'Are you kidding? Yes! I'd love to hook up. Where and when?'*

After replying, he put his phone away. A smile spread across his face.

'That bitch is going to get hers, right?' Mr Tickles asked.

Simone nodded and whispered, "You can count on it!"

'I can't wait to see her naked, bleeding and screaming!'

"Yes, Father. She let me down, too – in fact, she was the one that drove me to hurting people. She broke me. Caused me to snap."

"Dear, dear. It sounds as though you have had bad experiences with women, my child. Can that justify your actions? I'm not so sure. But I say unto you, that ye resist not evil; but whosoever shall smite thee on thy right cheek, turn to him the other also. And if any man will sue thee at the law, and take away thy coat, let him have thy cloak also!"

"I'm weak, Father."

"Yes, my child. A lot of His lambs are. And when they are lost and scared, he welcomes them into his house. He will forgive you for your sins, child, but you *must* do the right thing to warrant his forgiveness. Confessing all your sins to me alone will not save your soul from total damnation."

"Yes, Father. I know I must tell the police of my crimes.

His phone bleeped again. He opened his messages. *'I have something totally awesome to tell you!'*

Intrigued, he responded immediately, leaving the Father to waffle.

'Sounds exciting!' he replied.

Instantly, a response: *'It's a surprise, so I'm not telling you until I see you!'* *'What the fuck is that cunt up to, sir?!'* Mr. Tickles blurted.

"I have no idea, but she's not going to live to tell me – not once I get her back to ours!"

'Excellent, sir. Let it be known, you don't fuck with us!'

"...so you see, my child, by confessing all your sins, your soul will be cleansed by our Lord and master. Our saviour."

"But I've killed a lot of people, Father, and not just the girl from last night."

"Oh, child. Will you tell me about them? Will you confess it all to me, then go tell the police the same thing? Will you seek total redemption?"

"It all started when Chaos came along, Father. Like I said, I thought I'd found what I was looking for, but I was wrong. So very wrong…"

***

Whips and Chains – it was a club Francesca had told him about. At the time, it was one of the hottest new clubs in the city. It wasn't the sort of place Francesca was interested in, because it was too full-on for her liking.

She had liked the tamer side of dom and sub.

What you got with Whips and Chains was something a whole lot heavier, much to Simone's excitement. And now he wasn't with Francesca, or Porsche, he was free to do as he pleased.

And so he did.

The first opportunity he got, he went to Whips and Chains, but was not expecting to meet and fall in love with a woman he met on his first visit.

As soon as he laid his eyes on her, he knew she was the one – she came out of the pyro gloom inside the club like a wave of destruction. Her leather cat suit could be heard creaking over the loud music, along with the clicking of her heeled boots, which rode her thighs. Her long black-as-night hair flanked her pretty face, causing her ice-blue-coloured eyes to stand out. She had a bullwhip hanging from her left hip, with a crop holstered at her right. She didn't so much walk, but saunter. Stride, even.

All eyes were on her, and by fuck, she knew it.

She lapped it up.

Her body seemed to absorb the attention, which helped it move in that prick-teasing manner. All her curves danced and played to the awareness of the hundreds of stiff dicks that surrounded her.

Jaws sagged.

Offers of drinks, pleasure and being used as a whipping boy were given, but she ignored them all – her steely gaze had found him, and she knew what she wanted. She *always* knew what she wanted, and what she wanted, she got. *Nothing* got in her way.

If it did, she crushed it beneath her boot heels.

She was a ball-busting temptress that rode the high, searing waters of hell; she was as hot as the lava that carried her forth.

She was Chaos, and everybody knew that, bar him. But that didn't matter – he was about to find out everything there was to know about her as she got closer to him.

As she strutted her stuff, a smile spread across her face. He couldn't move. His breath had jammed in his throat, and his legs had turned to pillars of jelly. No woman bar his mother had ever had such an effect on him.

His face flushed. His cheeks felt as though bacon could easily sizzle on them.

Simone's cock grew so stiff, he thought he was going to faint.

When she stood directly in front of him, all five-foot-nothing of her, and said "Hi!", his dick exploded in his trousers – his hot spunk drizzled out of his pants and ran down his thighs.

He buckled and quivered.

She giggled, which caused his cock to keep on pulsating and shooting.

Simone reached a hand out and slammed it down on a table in front of him. His body felt flimsy; his knees knocked. Shocks of pleasure skipped through him, causing a trembling sensation only a raging sexual urge could provoke.

Her hand reached up and grabbed his bollocks. She lightly squeezed his package as she whispered into his ear, "If it's any consolation, you've made my knickers damp!"

"*Ugh!*" he groaned, enjoying the tightness of her hand around his bits, which did nothing to stop his ejaculate. It was starting to seep through the front of his trousers, much to his discomfort.

"Jesus, you come like a fucking racehorse!" she said. "I can still feel it pulsating out the tip of your dick." Her grip tightened.

"*Ahh!*" he groaned, getting onto tiptoes.

"You like that, don't you! Naughty beast," she said, giving his nuts a twist in her small, not-so-delicate hand. "Maybe I should rip 'em off? Make a eunuch out of you…How would you like to be my sissy eunuch? My ball-less little bitch?! By the feel of your package, you ain't packing much – not much of a real man, are you?!" she continued, her grip getting fiercer.

"No!" he gasped.

"No, *Mistress!*" she said, twisting his balls that extra bit harder, which took him to his knees. She followed, her grip not loosening.

"No…Mmmm…Mis…tress…" he managed with a warbled tone. He could feel tears beginning to form. Bile gathered in his throat, burning.

"That's a good slave! Would you like Mistress to take you home with her?"

He nodded. "Yes."

"Yes what?!" she said, giving his privates a savage squeeze and twist.

Tears streamed down his cheeks, his voice but a squeak. "Please, Mistress!"

"Good slave dog," she said, finally releasing her vice-like grip. "I'm glad you finally got the message," she whispered in his ear. "I exercise my grip daily, which I've been doing for many years now, and could easily pop your grapes. After all, I can almost crush apples! Be advised, do not cross me, sissy, for I will crush them to pulp if need be."

"Yes," he said, adding "Mistress!" as quick as he could.

"Good," she said. "Now, get me a drink, slave, then come and join me."

"Of course, Mistress."

For fear of losing his sperm factory, Simone got her a drink. It wasn't just fear, it was lust – he really liked her, even though her greeting was a little unorthodox. As he continued towards the bar, he was able to straighten up.

Small sparks of a smile crossed his face.

He was going to enjoy the night, thanks to his new friend.

His new madam had been true to her word. After several drinks and being used as her personal footstool, Simone had been taken to her home for a good cropping and whipping – she had beaten him until he had fainted.

As she unleashed on him, she had told him this was her way of breaking in her new plaything, her toy, which she liked to tease and wind-up at first – she liked to know if the nut could be easily cracked. And, if so, she would discard it without a second thought.

When he'd awoken from his unconscious state, he'd found that he was still chained in a starfish position inside her torture chamber, which was her converted cellar. Her *"Pussy Pleasing Palace"*, as she liked to call it.

As he hung there, which felt like weeks on end due to all the windows being blacked out, he started to think she'd forgotten about him, but he knew it was another test.

A test he was not going to fail.

As minutes turned to hours and hours into days, Simone's stomach tightened with hunger. His lips began to crack. He soiled the floor below him multiple times.

When delirium started to kick in, she appeared like an angel of mercy.

"Many would have been crying and begging by now, Slave!"

"How...How...Long..." he panted.

"Long enough, Slave," she said, undoing the cuffs at his ankles and then his wrists. "There's food and water over there for you." She pointed to a table close by. "When you've regained control over yourself, clean your mess up, Slave, then join me upstairs like a good dog."

From her tone, he couldn't tell whether she was pleased or displeased at his stamina and being able to put up with her hard tasks.

But he soon found out how pleased she was with him when she allowed him to eat her cunt, which was something she never authorized a brand new slave to do. They had to earn it, but most never got that far due to her brutal initiation.

Had things continued in the same vein, Simone had thought he too would have succumbed to her viciousness, but, thankfully, he'd earned his keep. His place, even. Rather easily, too, he'd thought.

After finishing his meal, Simone cleared the floor of his shit and piss, took his empty dishes up to the kitchen, and then joined his Mistress, who was waiting for him spread-eagle on her bed.

"Well, don't just fucking look at it. Eat it!" she'd barked. Never had he been kept on his knees for so long – he remembered thinking how numb her clit must have been by the time he'd finished. "You're a very good Slave. Mistress likes you. You're not one for breaking, are you?"

"No, Mistress. I will serve you for as long as you want me to." And he wasn't lying, either. In that short time, he'd fallen in love with her. He didn't know or care if the feelings were reciprocated, he just knew that she was his madam.

"What a lovely thing to say, my little wind-up toy."

"Thank you, Mistress. I hope I'm not bold in saying this, but you have lovely legs, Mistress. I hope you will allow me to worship them one day."

"Oh, is that what my little Slave likes?!"

"Yes, Mistress."

"Well, we shall see. First thing tomorrow, I am having your cock and balls locked away, Slave. Don't think you will be touching me with that thing of yours. All I'm interested in is your tongue and what you can do for me. Is that clear, Slave?"

"Crystal, Mistress. I would not expect it of you – I only want to please you."

"That's good to hear. If you're a good boy, which you're fast proving to be, then I shall from time-to-time take you out of your cage and give you a release. I may even parade around in tights and stockings for you. And, if you're really lucky, I will allow you to worship my legs."

"Oh, thank you, Mistress!" he said, truly happy and eager.

She allowed a smile to appear on her face in front of him.

"Well, this is promising, Slave. From now on, you will live with me – anything you need from your own home, do so tomorrow. After that, this will be your new place, Slave. You will be given the spare room, which is kitted out with a single bed. I also have a cage big enough to house you should you be naughty."

The next day, as told, he was allowed to return home to pack a few things, arrange his bills and was then outfitted with his very own cock cage – she'd been slightly taken aback by his knowing of such a device, but at the same time, it pleased her.

"Don't forget, you will only have this removed when I see fit to do so. Any begging, crying or otherwise will earn you a harsh punishment, along with having the cage kept in place for *much* longer," she told him.

The key to the device was then placed on a rope necklace, which she wore at all times. It dangled between her tits, which he constantly thought about.

As days turned into weeks, Simone found he was in bliss. He behaved, obeyed and found himself to be the most obedient sub servant he ever thought he could be. *Then again*, he thought to himself, *it's easy because I have the best Mistress.*

His loyalty and dedication to pleasing and pleasuring her was not unrewarded. She constantly reminded him how *excellent* he was at his 'job' and how *contented* she was with how selfless and caring he was.

Simone never craved, whined or drew attention to his needs. No matter how hard his cock swelled within the confines of his cage, or how much his body sometimes shook with extreme horn, he focused on her.

Mistress Chaos was the light of his life.

He not only worshipped the ground she walked on, but licked it clean before approving her to step foot on it.

In his eyes, she could do no wrong. He didn't care if she did, or ever could, love him.

All he cared about was her keeping him around.

She was unlike anything he had ever encountered in his life, and maintaining her contentment meant everything to him. Her delight ensured he was staying put.

As the weeks turned into months, it looked as though they were going to be happily engaged in this relationship of Dom and sub for a long time to come.

With the passing of time, he got better and better at pleasing her – he sought out all her pleasure zones and could take her to a place beyond paradise. With this, she freed his cock from its cell more frequently and gave it the release it deserved.

Not only did she do this for him, but she also paraded around in skirts, stockings, tights, French knickers, hot pants, thigh-high boots and anything else he asked for.

Simone especially liked being told how much she "loved" her slave. That she was "blissfully happy to have such a delicious pet around."

He could do no wrong.

She never punished, screamed, or lashed out at him and always allowed him to pleasure her pussy and legs and make her feel comfortable.

After the first three of four years of their relationship, he had even earned himself a place to sleep at the bottom of her bed like a good dog.

But things soon after started to change.

By the time they'd been together five years, things had got sour. Little things began changing, such as being told he was no longer allowed to sleep on her bed, which were telltale signs of things not being as rosy as they once were.

His leg privileges and releases became less recurrent, until the former was non-existent; the latter became borderline extinct, too.

He couldn't work out what was causing these changes, but it upset him. He didn't care about the loss of bed and leg rights, nor did it bother him that he wasn't getting his orgasms. Well, not to begin, at least.

Simone still loved her.

Then the beatings started.

She would take her frustration out on him by locking him up in her *Pussy Pleasuring Palace* and beating him within an inch of his life. Mistress Chaos wouldn't just use a whip or crop, but chains, sticks and bamboo shoots – skin would be torn from his body.

Because there hadn't been any beatings until now, the pain had been unbearable to begin with, but his body soon toughed to it, so frequent the thrashings became.

He didn't know what he had done to deserve such treatment, and he was never told. Simone continued to go along with it all in the hope he would get his old Mistress back, but if anything it worsened, along with her moods.

She would also go out every weekend and not return. He would be left locked up or lashed to his bed.

It pushed him over the edge. It broke him.

She not only broke his body, but his heart, too.

His Mistress had let him down, and now he needed out.

Chaos would allow him to go so long without a release that Simone would feel delirious every time he was aroused.

When she realised he was not going to give her the satisfaction of breaking, Mistress started using other tactics to smash his spirit: ice baths, stringing him upside-down, lack of nutrition, making him stand outside in the nude from dusk until dawn, telling him to clean the floors with a toothbrush, parading him around on a collar and lead, along with many other things.

It never worked. All it did was make him hate. To resent her.

Simone started becoming insubordinate on purpose – he found pleasure in pissing her off to the point where she would scream, yell, curse and lash out at him in sheer anger and frustration.

Then she began bringing different men home.

Mistress Chaos was now visiting Whips and Chains throughout the week, not just on the weekend. Whenever she brought a new slave home, Simone would be forced to watch as the slave got to fuck her – something he had never been allowed to do. Something she had told him no slave had ever been granted the right to do.

She'd become so low that she was willing to sacrifice her own rule to make him suffer.

Mistress had also told him that she would never, ever allow him to leave her care until he was a broken, stuttering and crying wreck of a man.

When she occasionally let him out of the house, he thought about running away, but he never could. And, much to his annoyance, he knew she knew that. Mistress had him under her spell, and not just her lock and key.

But he knew something had to be done, and so, on a rare night out, Simone decided he'd had enough. He could no longer go on living like this. His sanity, what was left of it, was on the cusp of dropping into a black hole. He knew he wasn't that stable of mind, and now that he had lost another love of his life, Simone was uncertain he could stop his understanding from tipping over the edge. If that happened, he knew he would be put on a path of total destruction.

And so, whilst out one evening, he'd come to the rational choice of reaching out for help. At first, he hadn't known whom to turn to, but it soon became clear.

After seeing a flier advertising a Samaritan's hotline, Simone knew it was his only chance at getting out from under the black cloud above him.

"There's always help at the end of a line, right?" he said, snatching the mini poster from off the lamppost it had been glued to.

As he entered the numbers into a payphone on the outskirts of the town's fair, Simone's heart raced. His mind ran amok.

What if a bloke answers? I'm not telling no guy about all this!

What if the person is old?

What if I say too much and the person goes blabbing to someone else, such as the police?

After hanging up on a few operators, Simone was about to give up, then *She* answered. She with the soft voice of an angel...

***

"Who is this *she*?!" the priest asked

'*She is the cat's mother, you boy-touching faggot. There are just too many up-hill miners in the church nowadays!*' Mr. Tickles said.

Simone sniggered.

"Are you all right, my child?!"

"Yes, Father. Just a sneeze."

"But I thought…"

"She is—*was*—Toni. The voice at the other end of the phone – the one I thought would save me."

"Ah, I see."

"Just like the rest, she let me down. She was beyond the final nail in the coffin, but she helped seal my fate."

"What did she do, my child?"

"I told you, I caught her in the arms of another man, after she swore her feelings for me, Father. She not only crushed my heart, but tore it from my chest. She flaunted her affections for this other in my face. Mocked me. Then, when I confronted her, she lied. Lied like the dirty, filthy whore she was!"

"You keep saying *was*, child…"

"That's right, Father. I do." *You want to know why; you fuck…?!*

"Why…" the priest's tone wasn't as strong – as fire and brimstone – as it had been.

"I killed her, Father. Slowly. It took nine months until she drew her final breath."

"Dear God!" Simone heard the priest say, which was followed by a series of whispers. "What did you do, my child?!"

"I cut her, Father. Firstly, I started with her feet, and then I gradually stripped each of her legs to the bone over a period of time and feasted on her flesh. She tasted good."

"*Ohh…*"

"After hearing about a cannibalistic kink, I just had to give it a go. After nine months, I'd practically picked her clean. I then cut her into sections, harvested the organs, and buried the remains on the beach."

"Sweet Jesus!"

"Something like that, yes. She tasted good – I would have thought a liar would have had a rotten tang, but no. She was as sweet as she used to look."

"How long ago was this, child?"

Simone thought the priest sounded as though he was going to throw his lunch up.

"I buried her scraps a few weeks ago, Father. Since her, I've killed six young girls, two women and a fella. The man was an accident – he caught me killing one of the women. I've come under suspicion from the police, but they are yet to press charges."

"Now you've told me, you must go further to cleanse your soul and to seek total absolution, son!"

"Yes, I plan to, Father. I see no other way out of the situation I am in. I've been very bad, I know. But it wasn't all my fault. My biggest mistake, and regret, was allowing that bitch Chaos to break me. Once broken, I should have left, but I stood defiant to her abuse – I didn't want her to think she had won. That she had crushed my resilience."

"My poor child.

"It's my own doing, Father."

"Who else have you killed?"

"I don't know if I want to go into it."

"Please, my child – if you seek amnesty, then you must get everything off your chest. Do you remember the names of your latest victims?"

"No, Father. I don't remember any of the ones from my past, either. All I remember is, I killed two young teenage girls, a man walking his dog, four university students, Chaos, a Jehovah witness, and Toni…If there's more, I can't remember. My mind is a cesspit, Father. I didn't want this life of debauch. It was thrust upon me from a young age."

"Yes, my child. I see that. But now you are doing the right thing. Please, don't stop here. Go forth and unburden yourself, I beg of you!"

"I intend to, Father. If I don't, and nobody catches me, then I will keep on killing. I know I'll never be able to stop."

His phone bleeped. It was Chrissy – *'I just wanted to let you know that I'm at the Klitty. Can't wait to see you later. X'*

'That bitch has to have hers!' Mr. Tickles said.

"Go now, my child. Strike whilst the iron is at its hottest!"

"Thanks for listening, padre," Simone said, exiting his booth with Mr. Tickles held close to him.

When he got back to his house, it was gone six, and so he knew he had a good few hours to kill before he had to leave to pick Chrissy up from work.

"What could be so important that she couldn't just text me about it, Mr. Tickles?!"

'I have no idea, sir. But don't let her fuck with your mind!'

"No, I don't intend to let her!" Although, deep down and tucked just underneath the need to kill her, Simone was actually looking forward to seeing her once again. It had been too long.

'*Maybe fuck her guts out first. You know, one for the road!*'

"That's what I was just thinking!"

'*Great minds, sir…*'

"Mm, yes."

'*Are you thinking of hearing her out first, sir?*'

"Not really, no. I want to hurt her as much as she hurt me! I'll firstly fuck her, and then fuck her over!"

'*Eat the bitch!*'

"Oh, I'll do more than that!"

'*The fucking cunt should have stayed away, boss. Or, if she was going to come back, why not stay silent – why did she have to go and drag up the past? She must want a short existence.*'

"Ha! Maybe. Perhaps she owes some nasty people a lot of money, and is hoping I'll do her the fuck in?!"

Simone and Mr. Tickles both laughed.

When midnight came, Simone left his house for the Klitty Kingdom. He arrived there and was waiting outside the back entrance for Chrissy at exactly ten past the hour.

Drunks and rabble-rousers passed the entrance to the ally in which Simone stood – they were cheering, shouting and spilling their chips all over the pavement as they zigzagged their way home.

"Fucking pissheads!" Simone said, smiling as he watched the crowds of men and women stagger by. "Chucking out time is certainly something to see around here," he uttered.

He placed his hands inside his pocket and lightly stamped his feet to try and keep warm. "Come on, where the hell are you?!"

Then his fingers brushed against the large blade he had inside his left jacket pocket. It was his butcher knife that he usually kept in a wooden block by his microwave.

The inches of steel had gleamed when he'd removed it from its home.

"I'll cut her open like a warm loaf of bread. Maybe I'll do it here, or maybe I'll do it back at mine. Let's wait and see..." he told himself.

As a smile crept across his face, the stage door flew open – Chrissy burst out and screeched his name.

"Simone! Oh, my God!" She ran down the steel steps and threw her arms around him.

She smelt good. Her warmth radiated through his clothes and seemed to melt his rage.

Passion aroused within him.

He wanted her.

Needed her.

Before he could attempt to remove the knife, she planted kiss after kiss on his lips. "I never thought I would get to see you again. Why did you stop sending me e-mails? I was scared you hated me. When I sent you that text this morning, I wasn't sure you were going to respond. I also thought that maybe you had changed your number."

"What if I had?" he said, pushing her lightly away from him.

"I would have come looking for you. I still remember where you live, Simone."

"You're kissing me and hugging me like you're my woman. I may already have a woman!"

"If you do, then what are you doing here?!" she asked, smiling. "Come on, don't be mean. I've been dying to see you. I've not been with another since you, Simone. I knew I would be back this way soon, so I was keeping myself. Plus, I have a surprise for you!" she said, barely able to contain her excitement.

"What is it?" he asked her coolly. At the back of his mind, all he could think about was what he was going to tell the police in the morning, once he'd dumped this bitch down at the beach.

I lied. It was me, not the one-armed man! he thought, smiling.

"I'm not telling you here, Simone! I thought maybe you would like to get some takeout and a few bottles of wine? What do you say?"

"I…I'm not sure, Chrissy. I mean…It's been a long time. I've changed. Moved on…" He knew he'd hurt her – the look in her eye told him everything.

"Oh, I see…"

Looking at her, Simone saw himself. *Is that how I appeared when I was crushed, time and again?*

"Look, maybe that was a bit harsh." His grip loosened on his knife. "Come back to mine. We can talk."

Her face regained its happy glow.

When they got back to Simone's house, he poured them both a glass of wine – he'd had reservations of spiking her drink, but he didn't want her numb to the pain he planned to dish out later in the evening.

"I was hoping you'd have been extremely happy to see me, Simone. Before I left here the last time, you were all over me. You were begging me to stay…"

74

"Yes, but you left, Chrissy. You left and you broke my heart. You let me down, much like every other woman in my life has at one point or another."

"If you felt like that, why did you bother keeping in touch for so long?!"

"I guess I was hoping..."

"Look, I'm here now. Why don't we try and get back to where we were?"

Oh, I'm sure you'd fucking love that, wouldn't you, bitch? Build me up, just to fucking smash me down again? he thought. His grip on the wine glass intensified, which put the stem under threat of snapping.

"Why don't you stop beating around the bush and tell me what this whole surprise is?"

"I'm not sure there's much point in me saying, now..."

He felt like throwing his glass to one side, removing his knife, and scalping her. Simone was about to do so – she must have seen the rage cloud over his pupils.

Putting her glass down, she picked up her bag.

She's thinking of leaving. Stop her! his mind yelled.

She removed an envelope from her bag, which stopped him from attacking. "Here, for you," she said, handing it to him. "I'll completely understand, of course..."

Setting his own glass aside, Simone looked at what he'd been given.

"Go on," she urged.

Ripping the envelope open, he removed what was inside. "What's this?" he asked.

"It's a one-way ticket to the States, Simone. I was hoping you'd come home with me at the end of my stay. I'll be leaving here in two weeks."

"But—"

"Before you say anything, I just want to say that you'll be fine living with me, and you won't have to worry about a job, as I've cleared it with the girls."

"Cleared what?!" He felt numb. Staggered. He didn't know what to say. She'd dropped a bombshell.

"To work the show with us – we'll figure out a role for you. You could put this place up for rent, right? Come on, what do you say? Throw caution to the wind!"

He hesitated. He'd sought absolution and spoken about his sins. Had his prayers been answered? Was this a sign from God? A message? *Go forth, child*, he heard his judicious Lord say. *Maybe I should*, he thought. He'd be in a new place, with Chrissy and her friends, doing a new line of work.

New thrills.

New kills.

And Chrissy wouldn't be the wiser…or safe from him.

A smile spread across his face. *I guess miracles can happen!* Simone thought, looking at Chrissy. "Yes, I'll come with you," he said. "You've made me the happiest man alive."

"Oh, marvellous!" she shrieked, throwing her arms around him.

"Before we go…" he told her.

"Yes?"

"I have to *kill* some time with an old priest," he told her, touching the blade in his pocket.

FINIS

WIND-UP TOY: HAPPY BIRTHDAY, SIMONE

Simone lay on his bed and stared at the ceiling. His mother's words from last night rang in his ears: *"This time four years ago, I was being rushed to the hospital. You were such a precious-looking thing, my special baby boy..."* she'd slurred, tapping a finger gently against his nose. *"You'll be a big boy tomorrow!"*

After a bottle of wine, she regularly got soppy with him.

It was a cute quirk of hers, which helped build a magnificent personality. Not just a personality, but a woman and a mother.

Every year, on the eve of his birthday at around nine o'clock, she would tell Simone of being rushed to the hospital and having to endure nine hours of labour, which ended with a breech birth.

"Aw, Mammy's special little soldier!" she'd supposedly cooed on having him placed in her arms.

From that day forth, Simone and his mother had been the best of friends. Sadly, she was his *only* friend. He'd never found it easy to talk to other children. To reach out and connect.

His classmates laughed at him. Mocked his silly accent. Due to him having an Italian father and a Welsh mother, they called him "half-breed", among other childish names. The girls pulled his hair. The teachers forgot about him.

And yet he liked school. Simone never let the little things bother him. He had a good home life, even though his father had left before he was born, along with a great mother and half-sister, Sian, who cherished the ground he walked on.

In Simone's eyes, that was all he needed.

Friends will come. One day... he thought, turning his head to look out his window. The curtains were wide open, which in turn allowed sunlight to filter through, causing him to squint.

His radio alarm clock, which was in the shape of the A-Team's van, burst to life – it pumped out the show's famous soundtrack. Simone sprang from his bed, and commando-rolled along the floor.

"I pity the fool!" he screeched, causing his prepubescent voice to crack.

When the A-Team's intro came to an end, a news broadcaster kicked in, informing him it was nine A.M, June 7th.

"*Ugh!*" Simone said, switching the contraption off.

"Are you up, love?!" his mother called from downstairs.

"Yep!"

"Hurry down, soldier - I have presents and pancakes ready and waiting! Get 'em while they're hot. The presents too," she said, laughing.

"Yes, pancakes!" Pulling his sagging PJ bottoms up, Simone raced through his bedroom door and downstairs. When he got to the entrance of the living room, the smell of buttery goodness caused his flat stomach to rumble.

Licking his lips, he walked into the room and saw the bunting his mother had put up on the walls: balloons, banners and streamers. He made his way into the kitchen, where he found his mother lathering his pancakes in syrup.

"I hope you're hungry!"

"Mmm, I am, I am!" he squealed.

"Do you want to open your presents as you eat?"

"I didn't think I would be allowed to..." he said, his words trailing off.

"It's your birthday, soldier. You can do anything you want!"

"Cool. Then yes, I'll scoff as I open. Where's Sian?"

"She had to go to school, silly!"

"Oh, I thought she may have been allowed to stay home with me..."

"Nope, just you and me, Simone," she said, smiling. After planting a kiss on his forehead, she then gave his nose a honk before pinching his cheek.

"Aw!" He giggled, wiping her wetness from his face.

When his breakfast was plonked down in front of him, he started stuffing large chunks of pancake into his mouth. Syrup trickled down the sides of his mouth and chin, causing some to dribble onto his pyjama top.

"Slow down! You'll choke, unless you're hoping to see the inside of an emergency room on your birthday?!"

Simone snorted a laugh, and chewed lumps of food spattered the table.

"Don't make me laugh!" he garbled.

"*Ew!* Mushy grub!" his mother bellowed, pointing at the debris that had come from inside his mouth. "Disgusting!" She then laughed and gave his bed-hair a tousle. "I'll get your first present."

With that, his mother was gone, leaving him to kick his legs, eat and hum "Happy Birthday to Me."

A silly, lop-sided smile appeared on his face.

"Look what I found!" his mother said, coming back into the room with her arm full of presents.

"*Wow!*" Simone said, spitting food chippings.

"Which one would you like to open first?!"

Looking at the brightly wrapped mountain before him, Simone was immediately drawn to the biggest one. "That one!" he pointed.

"Nuh-uh, soldier. No way. That one's from me and will be the last one you get to open."

"Is there one from Dad this year?"

"Surprisingly, yes! I guess there's a first time for everything."

"Awesome. Can I have that one first?"

She passed him his father's gift. Simone ripped the plain brown packaging off and instantly lost interest in the unwrapped present that sat before him. "Paddington Bear…*Really*?!" he said, looking at his mother, who removed the bear from the table.

"The less said about that the better!" she said. "Here, open this one – it's off Sian."

Eagerly, he tore the paper free from the parcel – his pancakes sat forgotten, the syrup hardening.

"Oh, wow – G.I. Joe action figures!" he said, showing his mother. "This is turning out to be the best birthday ever, Mam."

"I just wish we could have invited a few friends around..." she said.

Her words seemed to catch him off-kilter. All of a sudden, Simone felt like a loser. Did his mother think that? Simone had no mates.

He smiled a sad smile, but she didn't seem to detect it.

When he looked at her closer, he could see she had a sad way about her eyes. Her smile didn't quite fit her mouth.

Simone wanted to say something, to tell her he was fine in life, but words failed him, and as his mouth flapped, she pushed her present under his nose.

One corner was not taped down well enough, so he picked away at that section until a huge strip of paper came free in his hand. With the gift at his mercy, he savaged the rest of the packaging to reveal a massive clown.

The figure of fun bore black, reds and purples for colouring – his hair was huge and floppy. He didn't have a goofy red nose like most clowns. Its eyes looked sinister, its teeth sharp.

Simone was glad the thing was tied to its box.

"Don't you like him?" his mother asked.

"Uh..."

"Oh, I thought you would have loved him, being as you like all things horror and terrifying."

Simone couldn't answer. He was rooted to the spot. The clown's eyes felt as though they were boring through him. They were questioning and seeking out all his childish fears.

The urge to pee came from nowhere.

"He's cool..." Simone managed. His tone sounded shaky.

"Have you seen all the awesome weapons he comes with?" his mother said, pointing out the clown's mini arsenal, which was taped down: chainsaw, knives, hatchet, and axe. "Hey, he could be the leader of the G.I. Joes!"

Her words passed over him.

Finally, he broke the clown's intense stare and read the words arched across the top of the box: *Friends Until the End*! Blood dripped off each letter.

Friends...Simone thought. The word stuck in his head.

"Are you sure you like him?"

"Yes..." he said with caution. *I bet the clown can smell my terror.* Simone could almost hear it laughing as if tickled. "Mr. Tickles," he blurted, and then smiled. As he undid the ties around the toy, his mother cleared the paper away.

"I'm just going to throw this lot in the bin," she said.

'*Friends forever, sir!*' Mr. Tickles said into Simone's ear, which didn't startle the youngster.

"Do you reckon we can whip these G.I.s into shape?" he asked the clown. "You're going to be my number two."

'*Yes, sir!*'

Picking the packet of G.I. commandos up, Simone eyed their names. "I think we're going to have to rename these men. Give them some sinister sounding names."

'*Agreed, sir!*' the G.I.s said in unison.

Simone smiled. He finally had a group of friends to play with – his mother would be so proud.

"Who are you talking to, soldier?" his mother called from the kitchen.

"Oh, just my new friends!" he said, and then whispered into the clown's ear.

FINIS

WIND-UP TOY: PLAYTIME, SIMONE

"Well, if it isn't faggot chops!" he heard a voice call from behind him.

Simone knew exactly who it was – Cartwright. First name; Phillip-John – he was the most feared boy at Simone's school, but Simone had taught him and his goons one hell of a lesson last year…*Some people never learn*, he thought.

"Thought it was pretty funny, didn't you, whacking me in the bollocks with a hammer? I spent months in the hospital because of you, you little fuck!" Simone heard the lad crack both sets of knuckles. "Payback is a bitch, right?"

Turning, Simone saw that Cartwright was on his own; he didn't have his two chimps with him like he always did. "Where are your bitches?" Simone asked.

"Gary has a permanent limp, thanks to you smashing his knee in."

"And Ricky?"

"He's lost use of his arm. Again, that's down to you, my friend."

Simone smiled, "Yeah, beating you three was funny – you acted like a bunch of pussies. Fancy three getting taken by one?" Simone said, watching in amusement as Cartwright's face turned a deep shade of red. "I told you never to speak of that day again, or I would make your life a misery..."

"Yeah, well, I'm not about to let some little fuck get away with breaking my balls, Simone. Prepare for the beating of your life!" Cartwright said, stepping forward.

"Are you sure you want to do this?" Simone said, slipping a hand inside his trouser pocket.

"Oh, I'm more than sure!" Cartwright said, stepping in to attack.

He was much taller and weightier than Simone, which made him sluggish. This gave Simone a chance to dig the miniscule squirt bottle out of his pocket and stick it in Cartwright's face.

Without hesitating, Simone squeezed the trigger and filled Cartwright's face with bleach.

"*Argh!*" the boy screamed, as the hot liquid burned and ate at his flesh and eyeballs. He hit the deck and placed his hands over his eyes, which sizzled. "You fucking bastard! What have you done?!"

Simone looked about him. There was nobody around, which was why he always chose the riverside path to walk home from school.

"Yell all you want, Cartwright!" Simone said, circling the fallen boy. "Nobody's going to hear your sissy screams!" He gave him a few hard kicks to the balls. "Manage to fix 'em, did they?"

"Ah, you fuck. Fuck you!"

"Well, keep talking to me like that, and I'm not going to call you an ambulance!" Simone said, smiling.

"I'm sorry, please! Call me one – call *someone!*"

"Call you a what?"

"An Ambulance!"

"Are you sure?" Simone mocked.

"Yes, please! It burns," he cried. "I want my mam!" he bleated.

"Looks like you've had an accident!" Simone said, looking at the boy's wet crotch.

"Ugh…" Cartwright wept.

"Okay, okay, what can I do for you?" Simone said, picking up a large stick, which he used to poke the boy with.

"*Ow*! Don't do that, call me an ambulance…"

"Okay, okay…Cartwright is an ambulance, Cartwright is an ambulance…"

"What are you doing, you little fuck?"

"Doing as you asked!" Simone said, before starting to beat Cartwright about his head with the thick stick.

He yelped a few times, as blood poured out of his nose, eyes and ears. Once bored, Simone took to the lad's ribs and stomach. After a few more minutes of pummelling him, Cartwright took his last gasp of breath, before succumbing to death.

"That'll fucking teach you!" Simone said. "Never will you bully me again."

Making sure the boy was dead, Simone rolled him into the water, and watched as the current carried him down stream. He smiled, then giggled, before running off to his safe place…

****

The floorboards creaked as he walked across them as quietly as he could…*She can't possibly hear me*, he thought. How many times have I done this? Not once has she caught me.

But deep down, Simone knew she knew.

And even deeper down, he knew she loved it, and she knew he knew that.

It was an endless game of Peep'n'Come-Play', which she loved as much as he did.

Did it bother her that he was a lot younger? Did it fuck!

And did it bother him that she was much, much older? Not a fucking chance. Had the boys in school known what he was getting up to with an older woman, he'd be in a coma from all the high-fives he'd receive.

Tits, arse and legs – that's all the guys spoke about at school these days. He supposed they were of that age, not that he was popular among his peers. But Simone didn't care about that, as he had a good home life, and a family that loved and looked after him.

Getting to his destination, Simone put Mr. Tickles on the floor – his toy clown loved this just as much as he did, as he lay on the floor besides him, and then removed one of the floorboards. This, in turn, exposed a hole in the floor, and when looked through, he could see directly into the room below him, which was her dance room.

"If she really doesn't know I'm peeping, then I'll be in for the hiding of my life, if she ever finds out!" he whispered to his clown.

Chill. You know for sure she'd love it. She has guys looking at her body every night of the week. Go with the flow man, Mr. Tickles said. *The bitch is hot for it…*

Simone smiled. "I guess you're right."

I'm always right. Now, have a good look, because I want a good fucking eyeful too, you little pervert!

Simone stifled a laugh. "I'm the pervert?" he uttered. "Yeah, right! You were the one who wanted to lick Sian's pussy!"

And you're telling me you never did? the clown said, his eyebrows raised.

Simone smiled, and tried to hide his blushes. "Well…Oh, come on, you know I did. I liked it when she used to play doctor and nurse with me. She used to make my dick go all hard."

Well, that's supposed to happen! Don't they teach you anything at school these days?

"Shh, or she'll hear you!" he whispered. "We'll be able to talk a bit louder once she puts her music on."

Fair point, the clown said.

"What's taking her so long?"

She's probably slipping into character…I hope she plays Amber. I love it when she does Amber and puts her stockings on. Makes my cotton cock stiff!

Again, Simone had to stifle a laugh, as he put his hands over his mouth.

Below, he heard a door bang shut.

Sounds like our girl has finally come to play…

"Oh, man!" Simone said, beaming.

The clown beamed back, but before he could speak, heavy rock music started thudding through the ceiling – Alice Cooper started singing *Poison*. When this happened, Simone lowered his head, and put his eye to the peephole.

He couldn't see her, just any empty room filled with dance mats and walls covered by mirrors. "I don't see her!" he said in a sulky way, whilst keeping his head where it was.

Give her a chance! the clown said.

As Simone was about to complain some more, he noticed the lights dim in the room below. This was followed by flashing lights, which were multi-coloured and piercing to the eye. Before he knew it, she was out in the middle of the dance floor.

"Oh, man!" he muttered again.

What? said the clown. *What?!*

"You're going to freak out when you see this, Mr. Tickles. Looks like she's Trash tonight!"

The punk?!

"The very one," he said, looking down at the woman before him.

Even though the lighting was slightly poor, he could make out every inch of her body and what she wore. She wasn't the tallest of women, but her legs were long; very long, in fact, which matched the length of her black, curly hair. She wore it down tonight, which flanked her pretty face.

As she danced energetically, her hair skipped and thrashed, which drove Simone wild. Sometimes, she wore a headband or scrunchy, which kept her feral hair in place, but not tonight – it was on full display, much like her body.

Even though she wore a body stocking, it was fishnet, and exposed every contour of her young, tight body. Her nipples could be seen poking through the holes in the flimsy fabric, which, in turn, gave him an erection.

Beneath the fishnet however, she wore nude-coloured tights, which gave her amazing legs a glossy, shine to them…Her feet were bare, making it easier for her to glide across the mats.

"Oh…" he groaned, as he tried to get his face closer to the hole in the ceiling. "This is much better than watching the girls at Bunnies, Mr. Tickles!"

Let me see, you little pervert!

"Wait your turn!"

Did you see her oil her body?

"No, but maybe she didn't do it tonight."

True. I just love watching her oil those tiny tits of hers...

"Her nipples are hard, Mr. Tickles."

Oh... Come on, let me have a peep, Simone. Please!

"Just a few more minutes, okay?"

Fine, the clown huffed.

"No need to pout!" Simone said, giggling.

When *Poison* came to an end, the silence weighed heavily. Simone tried not to move, for fear of causing a creak in the boards. With a held breath, he pulled his face away from the hole.

Shh! he mouthed to the clown, putting a finger to his lips.

"*Phew*, that's loosened me up!" came the woman's voice.

Mr. Tickles sniggered at this, causing Simone to smother a laugh.

Putting his head back to the hole, he noticed she was now standing by one of the mirrors, while holding on to one of the bars affixed to it. In one quick movement, she put one leg up on it, and did a few stretches.

Simone's breathing started to come in ragged rips, as he watched her rub her leg, before putting it down and doing the same with the other. "Break the oil out..." he whispered, but she didn't.

After a few more moments of stretching, another rock song kicked in, causing her to start dancing around again. This song was much slower, so she used the pole that was situated in the centre of the room.

She rubbed against it, as she danced flirtatiously, before jumping on it and wrapping her legs around it.

"She can't half move!"

She's gorgeous... the clown said.

"I think her routine might be coming to the end."

Let me get in there, then!

Thinking they had plenty of time to switch position, Simone rolled out of the way for Mr. Tickles to get in to his place, but the music stopped, just before they could complete their task. A few boards creaked, causing Simone to wince.

"*Shit!*" he whispered. "Did she hear us?"

She's looking around...

"Oh, fuck – we're so screwed."

I think we're fine, Simone. She's now towelling her body down.

"Thank God!"

Oh, no...She's looking up!

"Let me see!" Simone said, moving the clown out of the way. Sure enough, the dancer was looking up at the ceiling. Her words tore through him, causing his dick to go limp.

"I know you're up there, Simone. I hope you enjoyed the show? If you're a good boy, then maybe I'll take you back to Bunnies. You'd like that, wouldn't you?"

He kept quiet.

"There's no need to be shy. I know what you get up to. Why don't you come down, so we can have a bath together? I'll let you scrub my sweaty back," she said, giggling. "Come on, there's no need to be shy. I'm not mad with you, you know that."

"You promise?" he asked, looking through his peephole.

"I promise, silly. Now come down at once."

"Okay," he said, abandoning his position. *What an interesting day I'm having so far*, he thought. *All this playing and sneaking around...But how am I going to explain all this blood up my arms? I could just tell her. I doubt she'll be mad...*

****

In the bath, they faced one another and looked lovingly into each other's eyes, as steam rose between them. It misted the only mirror in the room, along with the small window. He was down by the taps, with Mr. Tickles on the floor beside him.

It's only right that the man should be down by the taps, when you're in the bath with a lady, he thought, as foam bobbed and filled the gaps between them. Bubbles flew towards the ceiling, as they played footsie beneath the surface.

"And you say that blood belongs to a boy who used to bully you?" she asked.

Dropping his head, he went shy. "Yes. But I needed to put a stop to him once and for all...He would have continued."

"It's okay, Simone. I forgive you, my love...Did you get rid of the body?"

Looking up, he smiled. "I pushed him in the river, and the current carried him away."

"Well done. But my, you're not half a naughty boy," she said, lovingly placing her wrinkling foot in his crotch, as her toes played with his shrivelled nut sack. "It's this kind of behaviour that got Sian in so much trouble, you know..."

"Will they ever let her come back?" he asked, then groaned with joy, as he instantly stiffened. The tip of his penis jutted from the water like a periscope.

"Maybe. But only if she's good, and you learn to behave, Simone. You're naughty!" she said, wrapping her toes around his cock.

"Who did you say is the naughty one?" he said, and smiled.

"You can never, ever tell anyone about this, Simone...Or I'll end up like Sian. I could never lose you."

"That won't happen."

"Sex with a minor is so very, very wrong."

Following suit, he placed one foot between her legs, causing her to groan as he hit the right spot. Her hair tickled his foot and toes as he burrowed deeper and deeper. This was their favourite of all places to spend time, but never had it been like this before. He knew she loved him, but he never thought she or he would go this far. After all, he was so much younger.

The spying had been innocent compared to this.

Sure, the bedroom was fun and cosy and all those other things, but he'd only ever done sex things with Sian. She had taught him many, many things, and not just in the house, but outdoors, where they were free to roam and take plenty of risks at the same time.

He and Sian had made love and played with each other in many places, to which they had never been caught. He tried to think of the most unusual place they had played, but couldn't, as she slid her foot up and down the length of his shaft. *She's trying to tease me into an orgasm*, he thought. *But no, not yet – I don't want to. I want to make it last.*

Blocking out the intense pleasure, he managed to think about all the places he had enjoyed himself with Sian.

Fucking inside a confessional box at the church had been a good one. Sian had muffled her squeals of delight as the man-of-the-cloth had sat next to her, trying to preach some good into her.

The train ride home from Cardiff had been another good one...Boy, had that been awesome. She'd masturbated him to a climax, as they sat opposite a hoity-toity couple from London. *If only they had known what had been going on underneath my jacket at the time*, he thought.

He tried desperately to think of more times with Sian, as his mind drifted back to the present...

Suddenly, his mind filled with the day Sian had been taken away from him, which hurt.

Shifting in the bath, he found a more relaxed position, as he tried to cast his mind back once more. But nothing except that awful day would come to him, now he'd thought of it.

"Did you enjoy my dance, Simone?"

His eyes burst open. "Yes, I did."

"What about Mr. Tickles?" she asked, causing him to blush. "What's the matter? You don't have to be shy around me, you know. We're close, you know that, don't you?"

"He said you're sexy. Much sexier than the girls you work with at Bunnies. He thinks you're hot, and very fuckable."

"*Simone!*"

"Sorry, but that's what he said!"

"*Tut*, I'll have to wash that clown's mouth out with soap and hot water."

"I'm not sure he'll like that, you know!" Simone said.

No, he fecking wouldn't!

"Simone, no swearing!"

"But it was Mr. Tickles!"

She gave him a stern look. "And what do you think? Do you think I look better than the girls I work with?"

"Yes. Your boobs and legs are amazing…"

"Aw, that's sweet of you. But you know, we can't go on like this. It has to stop, and you have to be punished."

"I know," he pouted.

"There's no point in sulking you know. That won't work with me!"

He looked up at her, his eyes falling on her gleaming tits – her nipples stiff. What would it be like to suck on them? Sian's tasted so nice…But now she's gone. Locked away. The thought made him sad.

"You're thinking about your sister again, aren't you?" she said. He nodded. "They'll never allow her to come back here. You know that, don't you?"

Again, he nodded slowly.

"Is it time for my punishment?"

"Yes," she said, a smirk on her face. "It's for your own good, Simone. You can play with the girls at Bunnies, but I'm off limits. This will be your last bit of pleasure from me."

"Okay," he said, resigning himself to the fact.

"I'm also going to padlock the attic, so you won't have your peephole any longer."

"*Aww!*" he whined.

"Simone!" she warned, giving him another stern look. "Hand it over, come on," she demanded, whilst snapping her fingers.

He knew it was time – there was no avoiding it any longer. He reached over to the soap dish and picked up the cutthroat that lay there. Her eyes lit-up, as he flicked the blade open and clicked it into place.

Handing it to her, she took it in her left hand, whilst she held his arm still with her right. She then started running the sharpened steel down various sections of his arm, before turning her attention to his other arm.

He clenched his teeth, and pulled his lips back over his gums, as pain tore through him. His blood trickled and flowed down his arms and into the lukewarm water, where most of the bubble had now gone. All that remained was crimson suds.

She increased the speed of her strokes at the sight of him touching himself with his free hand – his foot continuing to probe between her legs, making her moan.

They brought themselves to orgasms, as water sloshed and swished over the side of the bath in a violent manner, soaking through the mat, which was positioned beside the tub.

Spent, she lay there panting.

He jigged once, as a joyous spasm ripped through his body, before laying still; his arms running a river of red.

As the water settled, she spoke.

"Did you enjoy that?"

"Yes, mother, I did," he beamed.

FINIS

ABOUT THE AUTHOR

David Owain Hughes is a horror freak! He grew up on ninja, pirate and horror movies from the age of five, which helped rapidly install in him a vivid imagination. When he grows up, he wishes to be a serial killer with a part-time job in women's lingerie...He's had several short stories published in various online magazines and anthologies, along with articles, reviews and interviews. He's written for This Is Horror, Blood Magazine and Horror Geeks Magazine. He's the author of the popular novels "Walled In" (2014) and "Wind-Up Toy" (2016), along with his short story collections "White Walls and Straitjackets" (2015) and "Choice Cuts" (2015).

LINKS

Facebook: www.facebook.com/DOHughesAuthor/?ref=hl

Twitter: DOHUGHES32

Website: http://david-owain-hughes.wix.com/horrorwriter